First published in Great Britain in 2005
by HEADLINE BOOK PUBLISHING

First published in paperback in Great Britain in 2006
by HEADLINE BOOK PUBLISHING

A HEADLINE paperback

1

ISBN 0 7553 2725 X

Typeset in Times New Roman
by Palimpsest Book Production Limited,
Grangemouth, Stirlingshire

Printed and bound in Great Britain by
Mackays of Chatham plc, Chatham, Kent

Headline's policy is to use papers that are natural, renewable and
recyclable products and made from wood grown in sustainable forests.
The logging and manufacturing processes are expected to conform
to the environmental regulations of the country of origin.

HEADLINE BOOK PUBLISHING
A division of Hodder Headline
338 Euston Road
London NW1 3BH

www.headline.co.uk
www.hodderheadline.com

A
CHRISTMAS
GUEST

To all those who believe in new beginnings

'I do not accept it!' Mariah Ellison said indignantly. It was intolerable.

'I am afraid there is no alternative,' Emily replied. She was wearing a beautiful morning dress of pale water green with fashionably large sleeves and a sweeping skirt. With her delicate fair colouring the dress made her look prettier than she was, and, having married money, she had airs above her station.

'Of course there is an alternative!' Grandmama snapped, staring up at her from her chair in the withdrawing room. 'There is always an alternative. Why in heaven's name should you wish to go to France? It is only eight days until Christmas!'

'Actually it is nine,' Emily corrected her. 'We have been invited to spend Christmas in the Loire valley.'

'Where in France is immaterial. It is still not England. We shall have to cross the Channel. It will be rough and we shall all be ill.'

1

'I know it would be unpleasant for you,' Emily conceded. 'And the train journey from Paris might be tedious, and perhaps cold at this time of year . . .'

'What do you mean "perhaps"?' Grandmama retorted. 'There is no possible doubt.'

'So perhaps it is as well that you were not invited.' Emily gave a very slight smile. 'Now you will not have to worry how to decline with grace.'

Grandmama had a sharp suspicion that Emily was being sarcastic. She also had an unpleasant and surprisingly painful realisation. 'Do I take it that you are going to leave me alone in this house for Christmas while you go visiting wherever you said it was, in France?' She tried to keep her voice angry rather than betraying her sudden sense of being abandoned.

'Of course not, Grandmama,' Emily said cheerfully. 'It would be quite miserable for you. But apart from that, you can't stay here because there will be nobody to care for you.'

'Don't be absurd!' Grandmama regained her temper with asperity. 'There is a houseful of servants.' Emily's Christmas parties were among the few things Grandmama had been looking forward to, although she would have choked rather than admit it. She would have attended as though it were a duty required of her, and then loved every moment. 'You have sufficient housemaids for a duchess! I have never seen so many girls with mops and dusters in my life!'

'Some of the servants are coming with us and the rest are going home to their families. You cannot stay here alone at

Christmas. It would be wretched. I have made arrangements for you to go and stay with Mama and Joshua.'

'I have no desire to stay with your mother and Joshua,' Grandmama said instantly. Caroline had been her daughter-in-law, until Edward's death a few years ago had left her a widow of what Grandmama referred to as 'an unfortunate age'. Instead of settling into a decent retirement from society, as the dear Queen had done, and as everyone had expected of her, Caroline had married again. That in itself was indiscreet enough, but instead of a widower with means and position, which might have had considerable advantages and been looked upon with approval, she had married a man nearly two decades younger than herself. But worse than that, if anything could be, he was on the boards – an actor! A grown man who dressed up and strutted around on the stage, pretending to be someone else. And he was Jewish, for heaven's sake! Caroline had lost what wits she had ever had, and poor Edward would be turning in his grave, if he knew. It was one of the many burdens of Mariah's life that she had lived long enough to see it. 'No desire at all,' she repeated.

Emily stood quite still in the middle of the withdrawing room, the firelight casting a warm glow on her skin and the extravagant coils of her hair. 'I'm sorry, Grandmama, but as I said, there really is no choice,' she repeated. 'Jack and I are leaving tomorrow, and there is a great deal of packing to do, as we shall be gone for at least three weeks. You had best take a good supply of warmer gowns, and boots, and you may borrow my black shawl, if you would care to?'

'Good gracious! Can they not afford a fire?' Grandmama said furiously. 'Perhaps Joshua should consider a more respectable form of employment . . . if there is anything else on earth he is fitted for.'

'It has nothing to do with money,' Emily retorted. 'They are spending Christmas in a house they're renting for the holiday on the south coast of Kent. On Romney Marsh, to be exact. I dare say the wind will be chill, and one often feels the cold more when away from home.'

Grandmama was appalled. In fact she was so appalled it was several seconds before she could find any words at all to express her horror. 'I think I misheard you,' she said icily at last. 'You mumble these days. Your diction used to be excellent, but since your marriage to Jack Radley you have allowed your standards to slip . . . in several areas. I thought you said that your mother is going to spend Christmas in some bog by the sea. As that is obviously complete nonsense, you had better repeat yourself, and speak properly.'

'They have taken a house on Romney Marsh,' Emily said with deliberate clarity. 'It is near the sea, and I believe the views will be very fine – if there is no fog, of course.'

Grandmama looked for impertinence in Emily's face, and saw an innocence so wide-eyed as to be highly suspicious.

'It is unacceptable,' she said in a tone that would have frozen water in a glass.

Emily stared at her for a moment, regathering her thoughts. 'There is too much wind at this time of the year for there to be much fog,' she said at last. 'Perhaps you can watch the waves.'

'In a marsh?' Grandmama asked sarcastically.

'The house is actually in St Mary in the Marsh,' Emily replied. 'It is very close to the sea. It will be pleasant. You don't have to go outside if it is cold and you don't wish to.'

'Of course it will be cold! It is beside the English Channel, in the middle of winter! I shall probably catch my death.'

To give her credit, Emily did look a little uncomfortable. 'No you won't,' she said with forced cheer. 'Mama and Joshua will look after you very well. You might even meet some interesting people.'

'Stuff and nonsense!' Grandmama said furiously.

Nevertheless the old lady had no choice, and the next day she found herself sitting with her maid, Tilly, in Emily's carriage. It made slow progress out of the city traffic, then sped up as it reached the open road south of the river and proceeded towards Dover, roughly eighty miles from London.

Of course, Mariah had known the journey would be dreadful. To make it in one day she had set out straight after breakfast, and it would surely be midnight before they reached whatever godforsaken spot in which Caroline had chosen to spend Christmas. Heaven alone knew what it would be like! If they were in trying circumstances it might be no more than a cottage without civilised facilities, and so cramped she would spend the entire time forced into their company. It was going to be the worst Christmas of her life!

Emily's thoughtlessness in gallivanting off to France, of all places, at this time of year, was beyond belief! It was an outrage against all family loyalty and duty.

The day was grey and still, and mercifully the rain was no more than a spattering now and then. They stopped for luncheon, and to change the horses, and again a little after four o'clock for afternoon tea. By that time, naturally, it was dark and Mariah had not the faintest idea where she was. She was tired, her legs were cramped from the long sitting, and unavoidably she was rattled and jolted around with the constant movement. And, of course, it was cold – perishingly so.

They stopped again to enquire the way as lanes grew narrower and even more rutted and overhung. When at last they arrived at St Mary in the Marsh Mariah was in a temper fit to light a fire with the sheer heat of her words. She climbed out, with the coachman's assistance, and stood on the gravel drive of what was obviously a fairly large house. All the lights seemed to be blazing and the front door was decorated with a magnificent wreath of holly.

Immediately she was aware of the smells of smoke and salt, and a sharp wind with an edge to it like a slap in the face. It was damp, so no doubt it was blowing straight off the sea. Caroline had obviously lost not only her money but the last vestige of her sense as well.

The door opened and she came down the steps now, smiling. She was still a remarkably handsome woman in her fifties, her dark mahogany hair only lightly sprinkled with the odd silver at the temples, which had a softening effect. She was dressed in deep, warm red and it gave a glow to her skin.

'Welcome to St Mary, Mama-in-law,' she said a trifle guardedly.

The old lady could think of nothing whatever that met the situation, or her feelings. She was tired, confused and utterly miserable in a strange place where she knew perfectly well she was unwanted.

It was several months since she had seen her erstwhile daughter-in-law. They had never been genuinely friends, although they had lived in the same house for over twenty years. During her son, Edward's, lifetime there had been a truce. Afterwards Caroline had behaved disgracefully and would listen to no advice at all. It became necessary for Mariah to find other accommodation because Caroline and Joshua moved around so much, as his ridiculous profession dictated. There was never a question of Mariah living with Charlotte, the elder granddaughter. She had scandalised everyone by marrying a policeman, a man of no breeding, no money, and an occupation that defied polite description. Heaven only knew how they survived!

So she had had no choice but to live with Emily, who at least had inherited very considerable means from her first husband.

'Come in and warm yourself.' Caroline offered her arm. Mariah briskly declined it, leaning heavily on her stick instead. 'Would you like a cup of tea, or hot cocoa?' Caroline continued.

Mariah would, and said so, stepping inside to a spacious and well-lit hall. It was a trifle low-ceilinged perhaps, but floored with excellent parquet. The stairs swept up to a landing above, and presumably several bedrooms. If the fires were kept stoked and the cook were any good, it might be endurable after all.

The footman carried her cases in and Tilly followed behind him. Joshua came forward and welcomed his wife's mama-in-law, taking her cape himself. She was escorted into the withdrawing room, where there was a blazing fire in a hearth large enough to have accommodated half a tree.

'Perhaps you would enjoy a glass of sherry after such a long journey?' Joshua offered. He was a slender man of little above average height, but possessed of extraordinary grace, and the suppleness and beauty of an actor's voice. He was not handsome in a traditional sense – his nose was rather too prominent, his features too mobile – but he had a presence one could not ignore. Every prejudice in Mariah dictated that she disliked him, yet he had sensed her feelings far more accurately than Caroline had.

'Thank you,' she accepted. 'I would.'

He poured a full glass from the crystal decanter and brought it to her. They sat and made conversation about the area, its features and a little of its history. After half an hour she retired to bed, surprised to find it was still only quarter past ten, a perfectly reasonable hour. She had imagined it to be the middle of the night. It felt like it, and it was irritating to be wrong.

She awoke in the morning after having slept all night almost without moving. From the amount of light coming through the curtains it appeared to be quite late, possibly even after breakfast. She had barely bothered to look at her surroundings when she arrived. Now she saw an agreeable room – a trifle old-fashioned, which normally she approved of. The modern style of having less furniture – making far too much open space – no tassels, frills, carvings, embroidered samplers and photographs on the walls and on every available surface, she found too sparse. It made a place look as if no one lived there – or if they did, then they had no family or background they dared to display.

But here she was determined not to like anything. She had been put upon, dismissed from such home as she had, and packed off to the seaside like a maid who had got herself with child, and needed to be removed until it all could be dealt with. It was a cruel and irresponsible way to treat one's grandmother. But then all respect had disappeared in modern times. The young had no manners left at all.

She rose and dressed, with Tilly's assistance, then went downstairs, more than ready for something to eat.

Then she found to her fury that Caroline and Joshua had risen early and gone for a walk towards the beach. She was obliged to have toast and marmalade and a lightly boiled egg, sitting by herself in the dining room at one end of a finely polished mahogany table surrounded by fourteen chairs. It was agreeably warm in the house, and yet she felt cold, not of the body so much as of the mind. She did not belong here. She was acquainted with no one. Even the servants were strangers about whom she knew nothing at all, nor they of her. There was nothing to do and no one to talk to.

When she had finished she stood up and went to the long windows. It looked bitterly cold outside: a wind-ragged sky, clouds torn apart and streaming across a bleached blue as if the colour had died in it. The trees were leafless; black branches wet and shivering, bending at the tops. There was nothing in the garden that looked even remotely like a flower. An old man walked along the lane beyond the gate, his hat jammed on his head, scarf ends whipped around his shoulders and flapping behind him. He did not even glance in her direction.

Mariah went into the withdrawing room where the fire was roaring comfortably, and sat down to wait for Caroline and Joshua to return. She was going to be bored to weeping, and there was no help for it. It was a bitter thing to be so abandoned in her old age.

Might there be any sort of social life at all in this godforsaken spot? She rang the bell and in a few moments the maid appeared, a country girl by the look of her.

'Yes, Mrs Ellison?' she said expectantly.

'What is your name?' Mariah demanded.

'Abigail, ma'am.'

'Perhaps you can tell me, Abigail, what people do here, other than attend church? I presume there is a church?'

'Yes, ma'am. St Mary the Virgin.'

'What else? Are there societies, parties? Do people hold musical evenings, or lectures? Or anything at all?'

The girl looked dumbfounded. 'I don't know, ma'am. I'll ask Cook.' And before Mariah could excuse her, she turned and fled.

'Fool!' the old lady said under her breath. Where on earth was Caroline? How long would she walk in a howling gale? She was besotted with Joshua and behaving like a girl. It was ridiculous.

It turned out to be another hour and a half before they came in, cheerful, windblown and full of news about all kinds of local events that sounded provincial and desperately boring. Some old gentleman was going to speak about butter-flies at the local church hall. A maiden lady intended to discuss her travels in an unknown area of Scotland, or, worse than that, one that had been known and forgotten – doubt-less for very good reasons.

'Does anyone play cards?' Mariah enquired. 'Other than Snap, or Old Maid?'

'I have no idea,' Caroline replied, moving closer to the fire. 'I don't play so I have never asked.'

'It requires intelligence and concentration,' her mama-in-law told her waspishly.

'And a great deal of time on your hands,' Caroline added. 'And nothing better to fill it with.'

'It is better than gossiping about your neighbours,' Mariah rejoined. 'Or licking your lips over other people's misfortunes!'

Caroline gave her a chilly look, and controlled her temper with an effort the old lady could perfectly easily read in her face. 'We shall be having luncheon at one,' she observed. 'If you care to take a walk, it's wintry, but quite pleasant. And it might rain tomorrow.'

'Of course it might rain tomorrow,' Mariah said tartly. 'In a climate like ours, that is hardly a perspicacious remark. It "might rain tomorrow", any day of the year!'

Caroline did not try to mask the irritation she felt, or the effort it cost her not to retaliate. The fact that she had to try so hard gave the old lady a small, perverse satisfaction. Good! At least she still had some semblance of moral duty left! After all, she had been Edward Ellison's wife most of her adult life! She owed Mariah Ellison something!

'Maybe I shall go for a walk this afternoon,' she said. 'That maid mentioned something about a church, I believe.'

'St Mary the Virgin,' Caroline told her. 'Yes, it's attractive. Norman to begin with. The soil is very soft here so the tower has huge buttresses supporting it.'

12

'We are on a marsh,' Mariah sniffed. 'Probably everything is sinking. It is a miracle we are not up to our knees in mud, or worse!'

And so it passed for most of the next two long-drawn-out days. Walking in the garden was miserable; almost everything had died back into the earth, the trees were leafless and black and seemed to drip incessantly. It was too late even for the last roses, and too early for the first snowdrops.

There was nothing worth doing, no one to speak to or visit. Those who did call were excruciatingly boring. They had nothing to talk about except people Mariah did not know, or wish to. They had never been to London and knew nothing of fashion, society, or even current events of any importance in the world.

Then in the middle of the second afternoon a letter arrived for Joshua. He tore it open as they were having tea in the withdrawing room, the fire roaring halfway up the chimney, rain beating on the window in the dark as heavy clouds obscured even the shreds of winter light. There was hot tea on a silver tray and toasted crumpets with butter melted into them and golden syrup on top. Cook had made a particularly good Madeira cake and drop scones accompanied by butter, raspberry jam and cream so thick one could have eaten it with a fork.

'It's a letter from Aunt Bedelia,' Joshua said, looking at Caroline, a frown on his face. 'She says Aunt Maude has returned without any warning, from the Middle East, and expects them to put her up for Christmas. But it's quite impossible. They have another guest of great importance whom they cannot turn out to make room for her.'

'But it's Christmas!' Caroline said with dismay. 'Surely they can make room somehow? They can't turn her away. She's family. Have they a very small house? Perhaps a neighbour would accommodate her, at least overnight?'

Joshua's face tightened. He looked troubled and a little embarrassed. 'No, their house is large, at least five or six bedrooms.'

'If they have plenty of room, then what is this about?' Caroline asked, an edge to her voice, as if she feared the answer.

Joshua lowered his eyes. 'I don't know. I called her Aunt Bedelia, but actually she is my mother's cousin and I never knew her very well, or her sister Agnes. And Maude left England about the time I was born.'

'Left England?' Caroline was astounded. 'You mean permanently?'

'Yes, I believe so.'

'Why?'

Joshua coloured unhappily. 'I don't know. No one will say.'

'It sounds as if they simply don't want her there,' Mariah said candidly. 'As an excuse it is tissue thin. What on earth do they expect you to do?'

14

Joshua looked straight at her and his eyes made her feel uncomfortable, although she had no idea why. He had fine eyes, hazel-brown and very direct.

'No, Mama-in-law,' he replied, using a title for her to which he had no right at all. 'They are sending her here.'

'That's preposterous!' Mariah said more loudly than she had intended. 'What on earth can you do about it?'

'Make her welcome,' he replied. 'It will not be difficult. We have two other bedrooms.'

Caroline hesitated only a moment. 'Of course,' she agreed, smiling. 'There is plenty of everything. It will be no trouble at all.'

Mariah could hardly believe it! They were going to have this wretched woman here! As if being banished herself, like second-hand furniture, were not bad enough, now she would have to share what little attention or courtesy she received with some miserable woman, whose own family could not endure her. They would have to cater to her needs and no doubt listen to endless, pointless stories of whatever benighted spot she had been in. It was all really far too much.

'I have a headache,' she announced, and rose to her feet. 'I shall go and lie down in my room.' She stumped over to the door, deliberately leaning heavily on her stick, which actually she did not require.

'Good idea,' Caroline agreed tartly. 'Dinner will be at eight.'

Mariah could not immediately make up her mind whether

to be an hour early, or fifteen minutes late. Perhaps early would be better. If she were late they were just rude enough to start without her, and she would miss the soup.

Maude Barrington arrived the following morning, alighting from the carriage that had brought her, and walking with an easy step up to the front door, where Joshua and Caroline were waiting for her. Mariah had chosen to watch from the withdrawing-room window where she had an excellent view, without either seeming inquisitive, which was so vulgar, or having to pretend to be pleased and welcoming, which would be farcical. She was furious.

Maude was quite tall and unbecomingly square-shouldered. A gentle curve would have been better, more feminine. Her hair appeared to be of no particular colour but at least there was plenty of it – at the moment far too much poking out from underneath a hat that might have been fashionable once, but was now a disaster. She wore a travelling costume that looked as if it had been traipsed around most of the world, especially the hot and dusty parts, and had no distinguishable shape or colour left.

Maude herself can never have been pretty – her features were too strong. Her mouth in particular was anything but dainty. It was impossible to judge accurately how old she was, other than between fifty and sixty. Her stride was that of a young woman – or perhaps a young man would have been more accurate. Her skin was appalling! Either no one

16

had ever told her not to sit in the sun, or she had totally ignored them. It was positively weather-beaten, burned and a most unfortunate shade of ruddy brown. Heaven only knew where she had been! She looked like a native! No wonder her family did not want her there at Christmas. They might wish to entertain guests, and they could hardly lock her away.

But it was monstrous that they should wish her on Joshua and Caroline, not to mention their guest!

She heard voices in the hallway, and then footsteps up the stairs. No doubt at luncheon she would meet this miserable woman and have to be civil to her.

And so it turned out. One would have expected in the circumstances that the wretched creature would have remained silent, and spoken only when invited to do so. On the contrary, she engaged in conversation in answer to the merest question, and where a word or two would have been quite sufficient.

'I understand you have just returned from abroad,' Caroline said courteously. 'I hope it was pleasant?' She left it open for an easy dismissal if it were not a subject Maude wished to discuss.

But apparently it was. A broad smile lit Maude's face, bringing life to her eyes, even passion. 'It was marvellous!' she said, her voice vibrant. 'The world is more terrible and beautiful than we can possibly imagine, or believe, even after one has seen great stretches of it. There are always new shocks and new miracles around each corner.'

'Were you away long?' Caroline asked, apparently forgetting what Joshua had told her. Perhaps she did not wish to appear to Maude as if they had been discussing her.

Maude smiled, showing excellent teeth, even though her mouth was much too big. 'Forty years,' she replied. 'I fell in love.'

Caroline clearly did not know what to make of that. Maude's hands were innocent of rings and she had introduced herself by her maiden name. The only decent thing to do would have been to avoid the subject, but she had made that impossible. No wonder they had found it intolerable to have her at home. Really, this imposition was too much!

Maude glanced at Mariah, and cannot have failed to see the disapproval in her face. 'In love with the desert,' she explained lightly. 'And cities like Marrakesh. Have you ever been to a Muslim city in Africa, Mrs Ellison?'

Mariah was outraged. 'Certainly not!' she snapped. The question was ridiculous. What decent English woman would do such a thing?

Maude was not to be stopped. She leaned forward over the table, soup forgotten. 'It is flat, an oasis facing the Atlas Mountains, and stretches out from the great red tower of the Koutoubia to the blue-palmed fringes and the sands beyond. The Almoravid princes who founded it came with their hordes from the black desert of Senegal, and built palaces of beauty to rival anything on earth.'

Caroline and Joshua forgot their soup also.

'They imported masters of chiselled plaster, gilded cedar and ceramic mosaics,' Maude continued. 'They created garden beyond garden, courts that led to the other courts and apartments, some high in the sunlight, others deep within walls and shadows and running water.' She smiled at some inner delight. 'One can walk in the green gloom of a cypress garden. Or breathe in the cool sweetness of a tunnel of jasmine where the light is soft and ever whispering with the sound of water and the murmur of pigeons as they preen themselves. There are alabaster urns, light through jewelled glass, and vermilion doors painted with arabesques in gold.' She stopped for a moment to draw breath.

Mariah felt excluded from this magic that Maude had seen, and from the table where Joshua and Caroline hung on every word. She was totally unnecessary here. She wanted to dismiss it all as foreign, and completely vulgar, but deeply against her will she was fascinated. Naturally she would not dream of saying so.

'And you were allowed to see all these things?' Caroline said in amazement.

'I lived there, for a while,' Maude answered, her eyes bright with memory. 'It was a superb time, something marvellous or terrible every week. I have never been more intensely alive! The world is so beautiful sometimes I felt as if I could hardly bear it. One gazes at things that hurt with the passion of their loveliness.' She smiled but her eyes were misted with tears. 'Dusk in a Persian garden, the sun's fire dying on the mountains in purple and umber and rose; the call of the little owls in the coolness of the night; dimpled water over old stones; the perfume of jasmine in the moonlight, rich as sweet oil and clear as the stars; firelight reflected on a copper drum.'

She pushed her soup away from her, too filled with emotion to eat. 'I could go on for ever. I cannot imagine boredom. Surely it is worse than dying, like some terrible, corroding illness that leaves you neither the joy and the hunger of life nor release of death? Even that exquisite squeezing of the heart because you cannot hold the light for ever is better than not to have seen it or loved it at all.'

Mariah had no idea what on earth she was babbling about! Of course she hadn't. At least not more than a needle-sharp suspicion, like a wound too deep to feel at first, narrow as a blade of envy, cutting almost without awareness.

What would anyone reply to such a thing? There ought to be something, but what was there that met such a . . . a baring of emotion? It was unseemly, like taking off one's clothes in public. No taste at all. That was what came of travelling to foreign parts – and not only foreign but heathen as well. It would be best to ignore the whole episode.

But of course that was quite impossible. The afternoon was cold but quite clear and sunny, although the wind was sharp. Escape was the only solution.

'I shall go for a walk,' Mariah announced after luncheon was over. 'Perhaps a breath of sea air would be pleasant.'

'What an excellent idea,' Maude said with enthusiasm. 'It is a perfect day. Do you mind if I come with you?'

What could she say? She could hardly refuse. 'I'm afraid there will be no jasmine flowers or owls, or sunset over the desert,' she replied coolly. 'And I dare say you will find it very chilly . . . and . . . ordinary.'

A shadow crossed Maude's face, but whether it was the thought of the lonely marsh and sea wind, or the rejection implicit in Mariah's reply, it was impossible to say.

Mariah felt a jab of guilt. The woman had been refused the comfort and sanctuary of her own home. She deserved at least civility. 'But of course you are welcome to come,' she added grudgingly. Blast the woman for putting her in a position where she had to say that.

Maude smiled. 'Thank you.'

They set out together, well wrapped up with capes and shawls, and, of course, strong winter boots. Mariah closed the gate and immediately turned to the lane towards the sea. In the summer it would be overhung with May blossom and the hedgerows deep with flowers. Now it was merely sparse and wet. If the wind were cold enough, after all her living in the desert and such places, the very damp of it alone should be sufficient to make Maude tire of the idea within half an hour at the most.

But Maude was indecently healthy and used to walking. It took Mariah all her breath and strength to keep up with her. It was roughly a mile to the seashore itself and Maude did not hesitate in her stride even once. She seemed to take it for granted that the old lady would have no difficulty in keeping up, which was extremely irritating and quite thought-less of her. Mariah was at least fifteen years older, if not more, and, of course, she was a lady, not some creature who gallivanted all over the world and went around on her feet as if she had no carriage to her name.

The sky above them was wide and wild, an aching void of blue with just a few clouds like mares' tails shredded across the east on the horizon above the sea. Gulls, dazzling white in the winter sun, wheeled and soared in the air, letting out their shrill cries like noisy children. The wind rippled the grass, flowerless, and everything smelled of salt.

'This is wonderful!' Maude said happily. 'I have never smelled anything so clean and so madly alive. It is as if the whole world were full of laughter. It is so good to be home again in England. I forgot how the spirit of the land is still so untamed, in spite of all we've done. I was in Snave so short a time I had no chance to get out of the house!'

She is not sane, Mariah thought to herself grimly. No wonder her family want to get rid of her!

They breasted the rise and the whole panorama of the English Channel opened up before them, the long stretch of sand, wind and water bleached till it gleamed bone pale in the light. The surf broke in ranks of white waves, hissing up the shore, foaming like lace, consuming themselves and rushing back again. Then a moment later they roared in inches

22

higher, never tired of the game. The surface was cold, unshadowed blue, and it stretched out endlessly till it met the sky. They both knew that France was not much more than twenty miles away, but today the horizon was smudged and softened with mist that blurred the line.

Maude stood with her head high, wind unravelling the last of her hair from its pins and all but taking her shawl as well.

'Isn't it glorious?' she asked. 'Until this moment I had forgotten just how much I love the sea, its width, its shining, endless possibilities. It's never the same two moments together.'

'It always looks the same to me,' Mariah said ungraciously. How could anyone be so pointlessly joyous? It was half-witted! 'Cold, wet, and only too happy to drown you if you are foolish enough to give it the chance,' she finished.

Maude burst into laughter. She stood on the shore with her eyes closed, her face lifted upward, smiling, and the wind billowing her shawl and her skirts.

Mariah swivelled round and stamped back on to the tussock grass, or whatever it was that tangled her feet, and started back along the lane. The woman was as mad as a hatter. It was unendurable that anyone should be expected to put up with her.

At dinner it was no better. Maude regaled them with tales of boating on the Nile, buffalos standing in the water, unnameable insects, and tombs of kings who worshipped animals! All very fashionable, perhaps, but totally disgusting. Both

Caroline and Joshua took hospitality too far, and pretended to be totally absorbed in it, even encouraging their visitor by asking questions.

Of course the wretched woman obliged, and all through roast beef, Yorkshire pudding and vegetables, then apple charlotte and cream, they were made to listen to descriptions of ruined gardens in Persia.

'I stood there in the sand of the stream splashing its way over the blue tiles, most of them broken,' Maude said, smiling as her eyes misted with memory. 'We were quite high up and I looked through the old trees towards the flat, brown plain, and saw those roads: to the east towards Samarkand, to the west to Baghdad, and to the south to Isfahan, and my imagination soared into flight. The very names are like an incantation. As dusk drew around me and the pale colours deepened to gold and fire and that strange richness of porphyry, in my mind I can hear the camel bells and see that odd, lurching gait of theirs as they moved silently like dreams through the coming night, bound on adventures of the soul.'

'Isn't it hard sometimes?' Caroline asked, not in criticism but perhaps even sympathy.

'Oh, yes! Often,' Maude agreed. 'You are thirsty, your body aches and of course you can become so tired you would sell everything you possess for a good night's sleep. But you know it will be worth it. And it always is. The pain is only for a moment, the joy is for ever.'

And so it went on. Now and then she picked at the

macadamia nuts she had brought to the table to share, saying that her family had given them to her, knowing her weakness for them.

Only Joshua accepted.

'Indigestible,' Mariah said, growing more and more irritated by it all.

'I know,' Maude agreed. 'I dare say I shall be sorry tonight. But a little peppermint water will help.'

'I prefer not to be so foolish in the first place,' Mariah said icily.

'Do you have peppermint water?' Caroline asked. 'I can give you some, if you wish?'

'I prefer to exercise a little self-control in the first place,' Mariah answered, as if the offer had been addressed to her.

Maude smiled. 'Thank you, but I have one dose, and I'm sure that will be sufficient. There are not so many nuts, and I can't resist them.'

She offered the dish to Joshua again and he took two more, and asked her to continue with her tales of Persia.

Mariah tried to ignore it.

It seemed as if morning, noon and night they were obliged to talk or listen to accounts of some alien place, and pretend to be interested. She had been right in the very beginning: this was going to be the worst Christmas of her life. She would never forgive Emily for banishing her here. It was a monstrous thing to have done.

* * *

Mariah awoke in the morning to hear one of the maids screeching and banging on the door. Was there no end to the lack of consideration in this house? She sat upright in bed just as the stupid girl burst through into the room, face ashen white, mouth wide open and eyes like holes in her head.

'Pull yourself together, girl!' Mariah snapped at her. 'What on earth is the matter with you? Stand up straight and stop snivelling. Explain yourself!'

The girl made a masterful attempt, took a gulping breath and spoke in between gasps. 'Please, ma'am, somethin' terrible 'as 'appened. Miss Barrington's stone-cold dead in 'er bed, she is.'

'Nonsense!' Mariah replied. 'She was perfectly all right at dinner yesterday evening. She's probably just very deeply asleep.'

'No, ma'am, she in't. I knows dead when I sees it, an' when I touches it. Dead as a skinned sheep, she is.'

'Don't be impertinent! And disrespectful.' Mariah climbed out of bed and the cold air assailed her flesh through her nightgown. She grasped a robe and glared at the girl. 'Don't speak of your betters like farmyard animals,' she added for good measure. 'I shall go and waken Miss Barrington myself. Where is Tilly?'

'Please, ma'am, she's got a terrible chill.'

'Then leave her alone. You may fetch Miss Barrington's tea. And mine also. Fresh, mind. No leftovers.'

'Yes, ma'am.' The girl was happy to be relieved of

responsibility, and of having to tell the master and mistress herself. She did not like the old lady, nor did any of the other servants, miserable old body. Let her do the finding and the telling.

Mariah marched along the corridor and banged with her closed hand on Maude's door. There was no answer, as she had expected. She would rather enjoy waking her up from a sound, warm sleep, for no good reason but a maid's hysterics. See if she liked the servants so much then!

She pushed the door open, went in, and closed it behind her. If there were going to be a bad-tempered scene over the disturbance, better to have it privately.

The room was light, the curtains open.

'Miss Barrington!' Mariah said very clearly.

There was no sound and no movement from the figure in the bed.

'Miss Barrington!' she repeated, considerably more loudly, and more peremptorily.

Still nothing. She walked over to the bed.

Maude lay on her back. Her eyes were closed, but her face was extremely pale, even a little blue, and she did not seem to be moving at all.

Mariah felt a tinge of alarm. Drat the woman! She went a little closer and reached out to touch her, ready to leap back and apologise if her eyes flew open and she demanded to know what on earth Mrs Ellison thought she was doing. It was really inexcusable to place anyone in this embarrassing position.

Gadding about in heathen places had addled her wits, and all sense of being an Englishwoman of any breeding at all.

The flesh that met Mariah's fingers was cold and quite stiff. There could be no doubt whatsoever that the stupid maid was correct. Maude was quite dead, and had been so probably most of the night.

The old lady staggered backwards and sat down very hard on the bedroom chair, suddenly finding it difficult to breathe. This was terrible. Quite unfair. First of all Maude had arrived, uninvited, and disrupted everything. Now she had died and made it even worse. They would have to spend Christmas in mourning! Instead of reds and golds, and carol singing, feasting, making merry, they would all be in black, mirrors covered, whispering in corners and being miserable and afraid. Servants were always afraid when there was a death in the house. Most likely Cook would give notice, and then where would they be? Eating cold cuts!

She stood up. She had no reason to feel sad. It would be absurd. She had barely met Maude Barrington; certainly she had not known her. And there was nobody to feel sorry for. Her own family had not wanted her, even at Christmas, for heaven's sake! Perhaps they were tired of the endless stories about the bazaar at Marrakesh and the Persian gardens, or the boats on the Nile and the tombs of kings who lived and died a thousand years or more before the first Christmas on earth, and worshipped gods of their own making, who had the heads of beasts.

But then her family could not have been nice people or they would not have turned Maude away at Christmas. They would have listened with affectation of interest, as Caroline and Joshua had done. Indeed, as she had done herself. She could imagine the water running over blue tiles in the sun. She did not know what jasmine smelled like, but no doubt it was beautiful. And to give her credit, Maude had loved the English countryside just as much, even in December. It was wretched that she should have died among people who were veritable strangers, taking her in out of charity because it was Christmas. Her own had not loved or wanted her.

Mariah stood still in the middle of the bedroom with its flowered chintzes, heavy furniture and dead ashes in the grate, and a hideous reality took her breath away. She herself was here out of charity as well, unloved and unwanted by anyone else. Caroline and Joshua were good people; that was why they had taken her in, not because they cared for her. They did not love her; they did not even like her. No one did. She knew that as well as she knew the feel of ice on her skin and the cold wind that cut to the bone.

She opened the door, her fingers fumbling on the handle, breath tight in her chest. Outside in the passage, she walked unsteadily to the other wing of the house, and Joshua and Caroline's room. She knocked more loudly than she had intended, and when Caroline opened the door to her she found her voice caught in her throat.

'The maid came and told me Maude died in the night.'

She gulped. Really this much emotion was ridiculous! She had barely known the woman. 'I am afraid it is true.'

Caroline looked stricken, but she could see from the old lady's face that there was no doubt. At her age she had seen enough death not to mistake it.

'You had better come into the dressing room and sit down,' Caroline said gently. 'I'll have Abby fetch you a cup of tea. I'm so sorry you had to be the one to find her.' She held out her arm to support her mama-in-law as she stumbled across the room and into the wide, warm dressing room with its seats and wardrobes and one of Caroline's gowns already looked out for the day.

Mariah was angry with herself for being so close to weeping. It must be the shock. It was most unpleasant to grow old. 'Thank you,' she said grudgingly.

Caroline helped her into one of the chairs, and looked at her for a moment as if to make sure she were not going to faint. Then as Mama-in-law glared back at her, she turned and went out to set in motion all the endless arrangements that would have to be made.

The old lady sat still. The maid brought her tea and poured it for her, encouraging her to drink it. It was refreshing, spreading warmth from the inside. But it changed nothing. Why was Maude dead? She had been in almost offensively good health yesterday. What had she died of? Certainly not old age. Not any kind of wasting away or weakening. She could march like a soldier, and eat like one too.

She closed her eyes and in her mind she saw Maude again, lying motionless in the bed. She had not looked terrified or disturbed, or even in any pain. But there had been an empty bottle on the table beside her. Probably the peppermint water. The stupid woman had given herself indigestion guzzling all the nuts, just as Mariah had told her she would. Why were some people so stupid? No self-control.

She drank the last of her tea and stood up. The room swayed around her for a moment. She took several deep breaths, then went out of the dressing room and back along the corridor to Maude's bedroom. There was no one else in sight. They must all be busy, and Caroline would be doing what she could to settle the staff. Staff always behaved erratically when someone died. At least one maid would have fainted, and someone would be having hysterics. As if there were not enough to do!

Mariah opened the door and slipped inside quickly, closing it after her, then turned to look. Yes, she had been quite right: there was an empty bottle on the bedside table. She walked over and picked it up. It said 'peppermint water' on the label, but just to be certain she took out the cork and sniffed it experimentally. It was quite definitely peppermint, clean and sharp, filling her nose.

Maude had brought it with her, with only one dose left. She must use it regularly. Stupid woman! If she ate with any sense it would not be necessary. Curious that they should have it even in Arabia, or Persia, or wherever it was

31

she had come from most recently. And the label was in English too.

She looked at it again. It was printed with the name and address of a local apothecary in Rye, just a few miles away round the Dungeness headland.

But Maude had said she had not left Snave, in fact not had the chance to go out at all. So someone had given it to her, with one dose in it. Presumably that was to treat the result of eating the macadamia nuts! But one dose? How very odd. Especially when they could have been all but certain that she would require it. Surely no household could be short of so ordinary a commodity, especially over Christmas, when it could be guaranteed that people would overindulge? There was something about it that was peculiar.

She picked up the bottle again and, keeping it concealed in the folds of her skirt, returned to her room where she hid it in the drawer with her underwear.

Then with Tilly's assistance – Tilly having rallied, her chill of little consequence compared to a death – she dressed in the darkest clothes she had with her – not quite black, but a grey suitable to a widow of many years, which in the winter light would pass for it. She went downstairs to face the day.

Caroline was in the withdrawing room before the fire. Joshua had gone to fetch the local doctor so that the necessary authorities could be satisfied.

'Are you all right, Mama-in-law?' Caroline asked anxiously. 'It is a terrible experience for you.'

'It was a much worse experience for Maude!' Mariah replied with tart candour. There were troubling thoughts in her mind, but she was not quite certain exactly what they were. She could not share them, especially with Caroline, who had never detected anything, as far as she knew. She might even wish to avoid scandal, and refuse even to consider it, and Maude deserved better than that! Perhaps it rested with Mariah Ellison, and no one else, to face the truth.

A few minutes later the doctor arrived and was taken upstairs.

'Heart failure,' he informed them when he came down again. 'Very sad. She seemed in excellent health otherwise.'

'She was!' Mariah said quickly, before anyone else could reply. 'She was a world traveller, walked miles, rode horses and even camels. She didn't speak of any ailment at all.'

'It can come without warning,' the doctor said gently.

'An attack that kills?' the old lady demanded. 'She did not look as if she were in that kind of agony!'

'No,' he agreed with a slight frown. 'I think it more likely that her heart simply slowed and then stopped.'

'Slowed and then stopped?' Mariah said incredulously.

'Mama-in-law!' Caroline remonstrated.

'I think it may well have been peaceful,' the doctor said to Mariah. 'If that is of comfort to you? Were you very fond of her?'

'She barely knew her!' Caroline said tartly.

'Yes!' Mariah contradicted her, equally tartly.

'I'm very sorry.' The doctor was still gentle. He turned to Joshua. 'If I can assist with arrangements, of course I shall be happy to.'

'Thank you,' Joshua accepted.

'We shall have to inform the rest of her family,' Mariah loudly. 'Bedelia whatever-her-name-is.'

'I have been thinking how on earth I can write such a letter,' Caroline acknowledged, 'what to say that will make it . . . "better" sounds absurd. If I simply say that we are terribly sad to inform them, will that be best?' She looked worried, and 'sad' would be no exaggeration. There was a grief in her face that was quite genuine.

Mariah's mind was racing. What was she allowing herself to think? Heart slowing down? Nuts that everyone knew were indigestible? One dose of peppermint water? Had Maude been murdered? Preposterous! That's what came of allowing one's granddaughter to marry a policeman. This was Caroline's fault. If she had been a mother of the slightest responsibility at all she would never have permitted Charlotte to do such a thing! Thomas Pitt was not a suitable husband. He had absolutely nothing to commend him, except possibly height.

But if someone like Pitt could solve a crime, then most certainly Mariah herself could. She would not be outwitted by a gamekeeper's son, half her age!

And if Maude Barrington had been murdered, then Mariah Ellison would see that whoever had done it was brought to justice and answered to the last penny for such an act. Maude might have been an absurd woman, and a complete nuisance, but there was such a thing as justice.

Mariah felt as if a light and a warmth had gone out of the air and a heaviness settled in its place, which she did not understand at all.

'You should not write,' she said firmly to Caroline. 'It is far too dreadful and sudden a thing to put in a letter, when apparently they live so near. Snake, isn't it? Or something like that.'

'Snave,' Caroline corrected her. 'Yes. It's about four or five miles away. Still well within the Marsh. Do you think I should go over and tell them myself?' Her face tightened. 'Yes, of course you're right.'

'No!' Mariah said quickly. 'I agree it should be done personally. After all, she was their sister, however they treated her. Perhaps they will even feel an overwhelming guilt now.' She thought that extremely unlikely. They were obviously quite shameless. 'But I will go. You have arrangements to make for Christmas, and Joshua would miss you. And I imagine I actually spent more time with Maude than you did anyway. I may be able to be of some comfort, inform them a little of her last hours.' She sounded sententious and she knew it. She watched Caroline's expression acutely. It would be a disaster if she were to come too; in fact it would make the entire journey a waste of time. In order to have a hope of accomplishing anything she would be obliged to tell

Caroline what she suspected with increasing certainty the more she considered it.

A spark of hope lit Caroline's eyes. 'But that is a great deal to ask of you, Mama-in-law.'

Of course she was dubious. Mariah Ellison had never in her life been known to discomfort herself on someone else's behalf. It was totally out of character. But then Caroline did not know her very well. For nearly twenty years they had lived under the same roof, and for all of it Mama-in-law had lived a lie. She had hidden her misery and self-loathing under the mantle of widowhood. But how could she have done anything else? The shame of her past continually burned inside her as if the physical pain were still raw and bleeding and she could barely walk. She had had to lie, for her son's sake. And the lie had grown bigger and bigger inside her, estranging her from everyone.

'You did not ask it of me,' she said more sharply than she meant to. 'I have offered. It is the answer that makes the greatest sense.' Should she add that Caroline and Joshua had made her welcome here and it was a small repayment? No. Caroline would never believe that. They had allowed her in; she was not welcome, nor was she stupid enough to imagine that she could be. Caroline would be suspicious. 'I have nothing else to do,' she added more realistically. 'I am bored.' That was believable. She was certainly not about to admit to Caroline, of all people, that she actually had admired Maude Barrington and felt a terrible anger that she should have been abandoned by her family, and very possibly murdered by one of them. She waited for Caroline's reaction. She must not push too hard.

'Are you certain you would not mind?' Caroline was still unconvinced.

'Quite certain,' Mariah replied. 'It is still a pleasant morning. I shall compose myself, have a little luncheon, and then go. That is, if you can spare the carriage to take me there? I doubt there is any other way of travel in this benighted spot!' A sudden idea occurred to her. 'Perhaps you fear that—'

'No,' Caroline said quickly. 'It is most generous of you, and I think entirely appropriate. It shows far more care than any letter could do, no matter how sincere, or well-written. Of course the coachman will take you. As you say, the weather is still quite clement. This afternoon would be perfect. I do appreciate it.'

Mariah smiled, trying to show less triumph than she felt. 'Then I shall prepare myself,' she replied, finishing her tea and rising to her feet. She intended to remain at Snave for as long as it required to discover the truth of Maude's death, and to prove it. Knowing alone was hardly adequate. Her visit might well stretch into several days. She must succeed. It was not a matter of sentimentality, it was a matter of principle, and she was a woman to whom such things mattered.

The journey was bumpy and cold, even with a travelling rug wrapped around herself right from the waist downwards.

There was a bitter, whining wind coming in off the sea, though now and again it cleared the sky of clouds. The light was chill and hard over the low-lying heath. This was the 'invasion coast' where Julius Caesar had landed fifty-five years before the birth of Christ. No such thing as Christmas then! He too had been murdered – and by his own people, those he had known and trusted for years.

Eleven centuries after that, William of Normandy had landed with his knights and bowmen and killed King Harold at Hastings, just round the coast from here. Somehow Mariah was faintly satisfied with Caesar coming. Rome had been the centre of the world then, and England proud to be part of that Empire. But William's invasion still rankled, which was silly, since it was the best part of a thousand years ago! But it was the last time England had been conquered, and it annoyed her.

King Philip of Spain's armada would probably have landed here too, if the wind had not destroyed it. And Napoleon Bonaparte. Only he went to Russia instead, which proved to be a bad idea.

Was this a bad idea too? Arrogant, stupid, the result of a fevered imagination? But how could she possibly turn back? She would look like a complete fool! To be disliked was bad enough. To be despised as well – or worse, pitied – would be unendurable.

Looking out of the carriage window as the sky darkened and the already lowering sun was smeared with grey, Mariah could not imagine why anyone would choose to be here if they did not have to. Except Maude, of course! She thought these flat, wide spaces and wind-raging skies were beautiful, with their banners of cloud, marsh grasses and air that always smelled of salt.

Perhaps she had not seen it frozen solid, or so shrouded in fog that you could not make out your hand in front of your face! That was exactly what would be useful now, Mariah decided: some dreadful weather, so she could not return to St Mary in the Marsh for several days. She had undertaken a very big task, and the more she thought of it the bigger it seemed, and the more hopeless. It was in a way a comfort that she could not turn back, or she might have. She had no idea what these people were like, and had not a shred of authority to back up what she was intending to do. Or to try. It might have been better after all if Charlotte were here. She had meddled so often in her husband's police cases, surely she had acquired a knack for detection by now?

But she wasn't here. Her grandmama would have to make the best of it by herself. Forward regardless. She had intelligence and determination, which might be enough. Oh – and right on her side as well, of course. It was monstrous that Maude Barrington should have been murdered – if she had been. But whatever the truth of that, her family had still turned her away, and at Christmas. That in itself was an unforgivable offence and, on Maude's behalf, she felt it to the core.

The distance was covered far too quickly. It was only a handful of miles, forty minutes' journey at a brisk trot, far less as the crow flew. Every lane seemed to double back on itself as if to circumnavigate each field and cross every ditch twice. The sky had cleared again and the light was long and low, making the shivering grass bright, and casting networks of shadow through the bare trees when the carriage drove into the tiny village of Snave. There was really only one big house. The rest seemed to be cottages and farm buildings. Why in heaven's name would anyone choose to live here? It was no more than a widening in the road.

She took a deep breath to steady her nerves and waited with pounding heart for the coachman to open the door for her. A dozen times she had rehearsed what she was going to say, and now when she needed it, it had gone completely out of her mind.

Outside in the driveway the wind cut like a knife-edge and she found herself rocking on her feet in the strength of it. She grasped on to her cloak to keep it from flying away, and stamped up to the front door, leaning heavily on her stick. The coachman pulled on the doorbell for her, and stood back to wait.

It was answered almost immediately. Someone must have seen the carriage arrive. An extremely ordinary-looking butler spoke to her civilly enough.

'Good afternoon,' she replied. 'I am Mrs Mariah Ellison. Mr Joshua Fielding, with whom Miss Barrington was staying, is my son-in-law.' The exact nature of their relationship could be explained later, if necessary. 'I am afraid I have extremely distressing news to bring to the family, the sort of thing which can really only be told in person.'

He looked alarmed. 'Oh dear. Please do come in, Mrs Ellison.' He opened the door wider for her and backed away a little.

'Thank you,' she accepted. 'May I ask you the favour of a little warmth and refreshment for my coachman also, and perhaps water for the horses, and at least, in the meantime, shelter from this rather cutting wind?'

'Of course! Of course! Do you . . .' he swallowed, 'do you have Miss Barrington with you?'

'No, indeed not,' she replied, following him inside after a brief glance behind her to make certain that the coachman had heard, and would drive round to the stables and make himself known.

Inside the hall she could not help but glance around. It was not a house of London fashion; nevertheless it was well furnished and extremely comfortable. The floor was very old oak, stained dark with possibly centuries of use. The walls were panelled, but lighter, and hung with many paintings, mercifully not the usual portraits of generations of forebears with expressions sour enough to turn the milk. Instead they were glowing still lifes of fruit and flowers, and one or two pastoral scenes with enormous skies and restful cows. At least someone had had very good taste. It was also blessedly warm.

41

'The family is all together, ma'am,' the butler continued gravely. 'Would you perhaps prefer to tell Mrs Harcourt this news in private? She is Mrs Barrington's eldest sister.'

'Thank you,' Mariah accepted. 'She will know best how to inform the rest of the family.'

He inclined his head in acceptance and led her to a doorway off to the side. He opened it to show her into a very agreeable room, lighting the lamps for her and poking up a fire, which had almost gone out. He placed a couple of pieces of coal on it judiciously, then excused himself and left. He did not offer her tea. Perhaps he was too alarmed at the news, even though he did not yet know what it was. Judging by his manner, he expected a disgrace rather than a tragedy – which in itself was interesting.

She stood by the fire, trying to warm herself. Her heart was still thumping and she had difficulty keeping her breath steady.

The door opened and a woman of great beauty came in, closing it behind her. She was perhaps sixty, with auburn hair softening to rather more gold than copper, and the clear, fair skin that so often goes with such colouring. Her features were refined, her eyes large and blue. Her mouth was perfectly shaped. She had very little resemblance to Maude. It was not easy to think of them as sisters. No one would have called Maude beautiful. What had made her face so attractive was intelligence, and a capacity for feeling and imagination, a soul of inner joy. There was no echo of such things in this woman's face. In fact she looked afraid, and angry. Her clothes were up to the moment in fashion, and perfectly cut with the obligatory shoulders and high crowned sleeves.

'Good afternoon, Mrs Ellison,' she said with cool politeness. 'I am Bedelia Harcourt. My butler tells me that you have driven all the way from St Mary in the Marsh with unfortunate news about my sister. I hope she has not . . .' she hesitated delicately, '. . . embarrassed you?'

Mariah felt a fury of emotion rise up inside her so violently she was overwhelmed by it, almost giddy. She wanted to rage at the woman, even slap her perfect face. However, that would be absurd and the last way to detect anything. She was quite sure Pitt could not have been so . . . so amateur!

'I'm very sorry, Mrs Harcourt.' She controlled herself with a greater effort than she had ever exercised over her temper before. 'But the news I have is very bad indeed. That is why I came personally rather than have anyone write a letter to you.' She watched intently to see if there were the slightest betraying foreknowledge in Bedelia's face, and saw nothing. 'I am afraid Miss Barrington passed away in her sleep last night. I am so very sorry.' That at least was sincere. She was amazed how sorry she was.

Bedelia stared at her as if the words had no meaning that she could grasp. 'Passed away?' she repeated. She put her hand up to her mouth. 'Maude? But she never even said she was ill! I should have known! Oh, how terrible. How very terrible.'

'I am sorry,' Mariah said yet again. 'The maid knocked on my door. I was in the same part of the house. I went to her immediately, but Miss Barrington must have died early in the night. She was . . . quite cold. We called a doctor, naturally.'

'Oh dear.' Bedelia stepped backwards and almost folded up into the chair behind her. It was a collapse, and yet it was oddly graceful. 'Poor Maude. How I wish she had said something. She was too . . . too reticent . . . too brave.'

Mariah remembered Bedelia's letter to Joshua saying that she would not have Maude in the house because they had an important guest, and she found it extremely difficult not to remind her of that. But to do so would make an enemy of her, and then gaining any knowledge would be impossible. Really this detecting required greater sacrifices than she had foreseen.

'I am deeply sorry for coming bearing such painful news,' she said instead. 'I cannot imagine what a shock it must be for you. I spent a little time with Miss Barrington and she was a delightful person. And I admit that to me she appeared to be in the most excellent health. I can understand your shock.'

Bedelia raised her eyes and looked up at her. 'She . . . she lived abroad for some time, in very harsh climates. It must have affected her more than we appreciated. Possibly more than she appreciated herself.'

Mariah sat down in the other chair, opposite Bedelia. 'She

44

spoke somewhat of Marrakesh, and I believe Persia. And Egypt also. Was she there for some time?'

'Years,' Bedelia replied, straightening up. 'Since she left, shortly before I was married, and that is all but forty years ago. She must have lived in a style far more . . . injurious to her health than we had realised. Perhaps she did not fully know it herself.'

'Perhaps not,' Mariah agreed. Then a thought occurred to her. Sitting here being pleasant and questioning nothing was unlikely to gain her any knowledge. Pitt would have done better. 'Or maybe she was only too well aware that she was not in good health, and that is why she returned to England, and her family, the people to whom she was closest in the world?'

Bedelia's magnificent eyes opened wider and were momentarily hard and cold as the midwinter sea.

Mariah looked back at her without so much as blinking.

Bedelia let out her breath slowly. 'I suppose you could be right. No such thought had crossed my mind. Like you, I imagined her to be in the most excellent health. It seems we were both tragically mistaken.'

'She said nothing that could lead you to expect this?' Mariah felt most discourteous to press the matter, but justice came before good manners.

Bedelia hesitated, as if she could not make up her mind how to answer. 'I can think of nothing,' she said after a moment. 'I confess I am utterly devastated. My mind does not seem to function at all. I have never lost anyone so . . . so very close to me before.'

'Your parents are still alive?' Mariah said in amazement.

'Oh, no,' Bedelia corrected herself quickly. 'I meant of my own generation. My parents were excellent people, of course! But distant. A sister is . . . is very dear to me. Perhaps one only realises it when they are gone. The void left behind is greater than one can conceive beforehand.'

You are overplaying it, Mariah thought to herself. You wouldn't even have her in the house! Outwardly she smiled. It was a totally artificial expression.

'You are very naturally suffering from shock,' she commiserated. 'When one's own generation passes away it is a reminder of mortality, the shadow of death across one's own path. I remember how I felt when my husband died.' So she did – the most marvellous liberation of her life, even if she could tell no one, and had to pretend to be devastated, and wear mourning for the rest of her days, like the Queen.

'Oh, I am sorry!' Bedelia said quickly. 'You poor soul! And now you have come all the way in this weather to bring this news to me personally. And I am sitting here without even offering you tea. My wits are completely scattered. I still have my beloved Arthur, now I must allow that to be my comfort.' She rose to her feet a trifle unsteadily.

'Thank you, that is most kind of you,' Mariah accepted. 'I must admit it has been a dreadful day, and I am quite

46

exhausted. I am so glad you have your husband. He will no doubt be a great strength to you. One can be very . . . alone.'

Bedelia's face softened in concern. 'I can scarcely imagine it. I have always been so fortunate. This room is a little chill. Would you care to come through to the withdrawing room where it is far warmer? We shall all take tea and consider what must be done. Of course, if you prefer to return to St Mary in the Marsh as soon as possible, we shall understand.'

'Thank you,' Mariah said weakly. 'I should be most grateful for as long a rest as I may take, without imposing upon you. And certainly tea would be very welcome.' She also rose to her feet, as unsteadily as she could without risking actually falling over, which would be ridiculous, and only to be resorted to if all else failed.

Bedelia led the way back across the hall to the withdrawing room, and Mariah followed, looking as wan as her natural dignity would allow. She must be consistent about her own exhaustion or she might be disbelieved.

The withdrawing room was spacious also and the warmth from the enormous fire engulfed them both as soon as they entered. There was too much furniture for more modern tastes: carved sideboards, heavily stuffed sofas and chairs with antimacassars on all of them. There were also hard-backed chairs by the walls with fat leather-upholstered seats and slightly bowed legs, and several footstools with tassels around the edges. A brightly coloured Turkey rug was worn duller where possibly generations of feet had passed. On the walls were embroidered samplers, paintings of every variety, large and small, and several stuffed animals in glass cases, even a case full of butterflies as dry as silk. The colours were mostly hot: golds, browns and ochre reds. Caroline would have thought it oppressive. Mariah was annoyed to find it very agreeable, indeed almost familiar.

The people in it were entirely another matter. She was introduced to them, and Bedelia was obliged to explain her presence to them.

'My dears.' Everyone turned to her. 'This is Mrs Ellison, who has most graciously come in person rather than send a message to tell us the terrible news.' She turned to Mariah. 'I am certain you would prefer to sit down, perhaps by the fire? May I introduce you to my sister, Mrs Agnes Sullivan.' She indicated a woman whose superficial resemblance to her was explained by the relationship. They appeared of a similar height, although Mrs Sullivan did not rise as the three men had done. Her colouring had probably been similar to Bedelia's in youth, but now it was scattered with more grey and the dark areas were duller. Her features were less finely chiselled, and her expression, apart from a certain sadness, was much gentler. Her clothes, although well cut, managed to look commonplace.

'How do you do, Mrs Sullivan?' Mariah said formally.

'And her husband, Mr Zachary Sullivan,' Bedelia continued.

Zachary bowed very slightly and replied. He was a slender

man with brown hair, now greying at the temples. His face also was pleasant, but marked by a certain sense of loss, as if he had failed to achieve something that mattered to him too much to forget.

'My daughter-in-law, Clara, and my son, Randolph,' Bedelia continued, indicating in one sweep a young man whose colouring resembled hers, although his features did not, being considerably stronger and blunter. The woman beside him was handsome enough in a powerful way: dark-haired, dark-eyed, and with brows rather too heavy.

Bedelia smiled, in spite of the occasion. 'And my husband, Arthur' she finished, turning to a remarkably handsome man whose dark hair was now iron grey. His eyes held a wit and life that captured attention instantly, and his smile at Mariah showed perfect teeth.

'Welcome to Snave, Mrs Ellison,' he said warmly. 'I am sorry it is distressing news which brings you. May I offer you tea, or would you prefer something more robust, such as a glass of sherry? I know it is early, but the wind is miserable and you have to be chilled, and perhaps tired also.'

'That is most generous of you, and understanding,' Mariah accepted, making her way over to the fire, and the seat Zachary had vacated for her. Whoever was guilty of having killed Maude, if indeed someone had, she hoped it was not Arthur Harcourt.

'What is it you have to tell us, Mrs Ellison?' Agnes Sullivan asked with a tremor in her voice.

'I am afraid Miss Barrington passed away in her sleep last night,' Mariah replied solemnly. 'I believe it must have been peaceful, and she seemed to be in excellent health and spirits right until the last moment. She made no remark as to feeling unwell. I am so sorry.' She glanced rapidly from one to the other of them, trying to judge their reactions. Not that she was sure she could tell guilt from shock anyway, or from grief for that matter.

Zachary looked least surprised, rather more puzzled, as if he had not fully understood the meaning of her words.

Agnes gave a gasp and her hand flew to her mouth in a gesture of stopping herself from crying out, oddly like Bedelia's five minutes before. She was very pale.

'Poor Aunt Maude,' Randolph murmured. 'I'm so sorry, Mama.' He looked at Bedelia with concern.

Clara Harcourt said nothing. Perhaps as one who had barely known Maude she felt it more appropriate not to speak.

Arthur Harcourt's olive complexion was a muddy colour, neither white nor grey, and his eyes seemed to have lost focus. What was he feeling? Was that the horror of guilt now the act was real and not merely dreamed?

'I am sorry to bring you such news.' Mariah felt compelled to fill in the silence from the others that seemed to choke the room. The mere flickering of the fire sounded like a sheet torn in the wind.

'It . . . it was good of you,' Agnes stammered. 'Such a

terrible thing for you . . . a guest in your house . . . a virtual stranger.'

Suddenly a quite brilliant idea lit in Mariah's mind. It went up like a flare and she could almost feel the heat of it in her face. 'Oh, not at all!' she said with feeling. 'We talked for hours, Maude and I.' She was stunned at her own audacity. 'She told me so much about . . . oh, any number of things. Her feelings, her experiences, where she had been and the people she had met.' She waved her hands for emphasis. 'Believe me, there are those I have been acquainted with for years about whom I know far less. I have never made such excellent friends with anyone so rapidly, or with such a natural affection.' That was a monstrous lie – wasn't it? 'I must admit her trust in me was most heart-warming, and indeed that was the reason why I could not possibly allow anyone else to come to you now,' she hurried on. 'I shall never forget Maude, or the confidence she placed in me regarding her life and its meaning.' She felt an extraordinary emotion inside her to have made such statements as if they were true, as if she and Maude had become instant and total friends.

She realised with a flutter of absurdity, even of sweetness, that it was not completely a lie. Maude had told her more of meaning in a day than most of her acquaintances had in years, although not the personal details she implied to her wretched family!

And grudgingly, like the lancing of a boil, she admitted

that she had actually liked Maude, at least more than she had expected to, considering the gross imposition of having her in Caroline's home for Christmas – uninvited!

Bedelia stared at her incredulously. 'Really? But you knew her for barely a day!'

'But we had little to do but talk to each other,' Mariah assured her with a smile. 'She was fascinating at the luncheon and dinner table, but even more so when we were out walking, just the two of us. I was very flattered that she should tell me so much. I found myself speaking equally frankly to her, and finding her most gentle and free from critical judgement. It was a quite . . . quite wonderful experience,' she added too quickly. She said it purely to frighten them into believing she knew something of whoever it was who had murdered Maude, if indeed they had. This was a deviousness added to her new grief. She intended them to think her too desolate to consider the long carriage ride in the dark to go home again!

She also found, to her dismay, that she wished quite painfully that it were all true. She had not been anything like such friends with Maude. Nor had she confided in her the agonies of her own life, the shame she had carried for years that she had not had the courage to leave her husband and flee abroad as his first wife had done! She could hardly call her wild and perfectly pathetic attempt to murder his stepson, before he could tell the world of her shame, a matter of courage. It had been farcical. She could still remember with scalding embarrassment her overwhelming terror that night, and her gratitude when he turned up shortly afterwards, no more injured than by an icy ducking in the dirty water of the Thames. She would have died rather than tell Maude such a thing! It was hideous enough that she could not remember now how much Caroline had known.

But it was startlingly sweet to think that Maude might have understood, and sympathised rather than despising her for a coward, as she despised herself. There would have been nothing in the world more precious than a friend who understood. But that was idiotic! Maude would never have submitted herself to such treatment. She would probably have acquired a gun and shot a man before she would have allowed him to do that to her!

'Then you grieve with us,' Arthur said gently, intruding across her thoughts. 'Please feel welcome here, and do not consider the journey back to St Mary tonight. It will be dark quite soon and you must be both tired and distressed. I am certain we can supply anything you might need, such as a nightgown and toiletries. And, of course, we have plenty of room.'

'Since Lord Woollard has just left, the guest room is perfectly available,' Clara put in quickly.

'Oh yes, the guest who was staying with you before, when poor Maude arrived,' Mariah noted. 'How very kind of you. I really should be most grateful. May I inform my coachman of your generosity, so he can return to St Mary? It is possible

Mr and Mrs Fielding may require the coach tomorrow. And, of course, if they do not hear, they may worry that something has happened to me.'

'Naturally,' Arthur agreed. 'Would you care to tell him yourself, or shall I have the butler inform him?'

'That would be very kind of you,' she accepted. 'And ask him to tell Mrs Fielding of your graciousness, and that I am perfectly well . . . just . . . just so grieved.'

'Of course.' Now the die was cast. What on earth was she thinking of? Her stomach lurched and her mouth was dry.

She sipped the excellent sherry she had been given and allowed herself to bask for a moment in its delicious warmth. She had embarked upon an adventure. That is the way she must look at it. She was still angry that Maude had been treated so appallingly, whether it included murder or not, although she really thought it might! And she was tired and grieved, quite truly grieved. Maude had been too full of life to die, too joyous in tasting every good experience to give it up so soon. And no one should be unwanted by their own, whatever the reason.

What was the reason? Who in this comfortable room, with its roaring fire, its silver tea tray and overstuffed sofas, had wanted Maude out of the house? And why had the rest of them allowed it? Were they all guilty of something? Secrets so terrible they would kill to hide them? They looked so perfectly innocuous, even ordinary. Good heavens, what wickedness can lie beneath a smiling exterior as commonplace as a slice of bread!

Later a maid showed Mariah to the spare bedroom. It was warm and agreeably furnished with a four-poster bed, heavy curtains of wine brocade, another red Turkey carpet and plenty of carved oak furniture. A very fine ewer with painted flowers on it held fresh water. There was a matching bowl for washing in and on the stand beside them plenty of thick towels with which to dry oneself. There was no way of telling that Lord Woollard, or anyone else, had occupied it recently. But she would take the opportunity to see how many guest rooms there were so she would know whether Maude could have been accommodated had her sister wished to.

Mariah tiptoed along the corridor, feeling like a sneak thief, and cautiously tried the handles and opened the doors of the two other rooms. They were both bedrooms, and both presently unoccupied. The lack of space had been a blatant lie.

She returned to her own room, her hands trembling a little and her knees weak. She sat down. Then another idea struck her. She opened the small cupboard beside the bed, and found lavender water, a vial with a couple of doses of laudanum, and a full bottle of peppermint water! The cork was jammed in tightly, but, more telling than that, there was a film of dust over it. It had evidently been purchased before Maude had left! That put a new complexion on Maude's single dose! Had there been something else in it, disguised by the pungent taste? And the macadamia nuts were given to make her require it?

Mariah closed the cupboard door and sat down heavily on the bed. So far everything had gone quite marvellously to plan – too marvellously. But there was a great deal to do. She must ascertain if Maude had indeed been killed, if so by whom, precisely how – and her investigation would hardly be complete if she did not also know why! How could she possibly do all that before they politely sent her home? Pitt had no challenge of mere hours in which to solve his cases! He went on for days! Sometimes even weeks! And he had the authority to ask questions and demand answers – not necessarily true ones, of course. She was going to have to be much cleverer than he was! It might not be quite as easy as she had assumed.

Still, so far, so good. And she was much too angry to give up.

However, later on, when in ordinary circumstances she would have been changing for dinner, she was overwhelmed by the strangeness of her surroundings and all the events that had occurred in the last few days. This time last week she had been in London with Emily and Jack, as usual. Then she had been upheaved and sent to St Mary in the Marsh. She had barely settled to accepting that when Maude Barrington had arrived. That was almost accommodated, and then Maude died, without the slightest warning of any sort!

Mariah had been the only one to perceive that Maude's death might well not be natural, but a crime, the most appalling of all crimes, and there was no one else but herself to find justice for it. And here she was, sitting quite alone in a house full of strangers, at least one of whom she was now convinced was a murderer. Added to that she had not even fresh under-clothes or a nightgown to sleep in. They had offered to lend her something, but all the women in the family were at least three or four inches taller than she was, and thinner as well, by more inches than that! She must have taken leave of her wits. Certainly she could never admit any of this to Caroline! Or anybody else. They'd have her locked up.

There was a knock on the door and she started so violently she gulped and gave herself hiccups.

'Come in!' she said, hiccuping again.

It was the housekeeper, to judge from her black dress, lace cap and the cluster of keys hanging from her waist. She was short and rather stout, exactly Mariah's own build.

'Good evening, ma'am,' she said very agreeably. 'I'm Mrs Ward, the housekeeper. It was very good of you to come personally with the sad news. It must have inconvenienced you very much.'

'Her death grieved me,' Mariah answered frankly, relieved that it was a servant, not one of the family. 'To come and tell you personally seemed no more than the obvious thing to do. She died among strangers, even if they were people who liked her immediately, and very much.'

Mrs Ward's face coloured as if with considerable emotion she felt obliged to hide. 'I'm very glad you did,' she said with a tremble in her voice. She blinked rapidly.

'You knew her,' Mariah deduced. She made herself smile. 'You must be grieving as well.'

'Yes, ma'am. I was a maid here when I was a girl. Miss Maude would have been sixteen then.'

'And Mrs Harcourt?' Mariah asked shamelessly. She must detect! Time would not wait upon niceties.

'Oh, eighteen, she was. And such a beauty as you've never seen.'

Mariah looked at the housekeeper's face. There was no light in it. She might respect Bedelia Harcourt, even be loyal to her, but she did not like her as she had Maude. That was something to remember. Servants said little, good ones seldom said anything at all, but they saw just about everything.

'And Mrs Sullivan?'

'Oh, she was only thirteen, just a schoolgirl, all ink and books and clumsiness, but full of enthusiasm, poor girl. The governess was always trying to get her to walk with the dictionary on her head, but she kept losing it.'

'Dictionary?'

'Only for the weight of it! Miss Agnes was perfectly accurate with her spelling. But that's all in the past. Long ago.' She blinked rapidly again. 'I just came to say that if there is anything I can get for you, I should be happy to.' She had an air of sincerity as if her words were far more than mere politeness, or even obedience to Bedelia's request.

'Thank you,' Mariah replied. 'I . . . I'm afraid I have none of the usual necessities with me.' Dare she ask for a clean petticoat or chemise?

Mrs Ward looked embarrassed. 'There is no difficulty in the least finding you toiletries, Mrs Ellison. I was thinking of . . . of more personal things. If you'll forgive my saying so, it seems to me that you and I are much the same height. If you would not be offended, ma'am, you might borrow one or two of my . . . my clothes. It would give us the chance to . . . care for yours and return them to you?' She was very pink; as if afraid already that she had presumed.

Mariah was suddenly touched by the woman's kindness. It seemed perfectly genuine, and perhaps enhanced because she had cared for Maude. 'That is extremely generous of you to offer,' she said warmly. 'I would be most grateful. I have nothing but what I stand up in. It was the last thing on my mind as I left this morning.'

Mrs Ward coloured even more, but most obviously with relief. 'Then I shall see that they are brought. Thank you, ma'am.'

'It is I who thank you,' Mariah said, startled by her own courtesy, and rather liking it. It flashed into her mind that in a way Maude's death had given her the opportunity to begin a new life herself, even if only for a day or two. No one here in Snave knew her. She could be anything she wanted to be. It was a dizzying sort of freedom, as if the past did not exist. She suddenly smiled at the housekeeper again. 'You have extraordinary courtesy,' she added.

Mrs Ward blushed again but it was obviously with pleasure. She retreated, and fifteen minutes later returned carrying two black dresses, an assortment of undergarments and a nightgown.

With the assistance of one of the maids assigned to help her, a most agreeable girl, Mariah was able to dress for dinner in very respectable black bombazine, well cut and modest in fashion, as suited an elderly lady or a housekeeper. She put on her own jet and pearl jewellery, serving the double purpose of lifting the otherwise sombreness of the attire, and also being classic mourning jewellery. She had a lot of such pieces, from the period when she had made a great show of being a widow. Added to which, they were really very pretty. The seed pearls made them dainty.

She went down the stairs and across the hall to the with-drawing room. She could hear lively conversation from inside, amazingly so, but she did not know the voices well enough to tell who they belonged to.

She opened the door, and they all ceased instantly, faces turned towards her. The gentlemen rose to their feet and welcomed her. The ladies looked at her, made polite noises, observed the change of gown but did not remark on it.

Conversation resumed, but stiffly, with a solemnity completely different from that before she had come in.

'I hope you are comfortable, Mrs Ellison?' Bedelia enquired.

'Very, thank you,' Mariah replied, sitting in one of the

overstuffed chairs. 'You are most generous.' Again she smiled.

'It is fortunate Lord Woollard left when he did,' Clara observed.

Mariah wondered whether that remark was made to convince her that they had not had sufficient accommodation for more than one further guest at a time, hence the need to turn Maude away. If so, it was ridiculous. She knew there were at least two more rooms unoccupied. And family should be first, most particularly when they were returning from a long time away.

'Indeed,' she said, as if she were agreeing. 'Is he a close friend? He will be very sad to hear of Maude's demise.'

'He never met her,' Bedelia said hastily. 'I do not think we need to cloud his Christmas by telling him bad news which can scarcely be of concern to him.'

So he would have no feelings for the bereaved family! It seemed they had entertained a mere acquaintance in Maude's place!

'I thought perhaps he was a relative,' Mariah murmured.

Arthur smiled at her. 'Not at all. A business acquaintance.' He sounded tired, a strain in his voice, a kind of bitter humour. 'Sent actually to assess whether I should be offered a peerage or not. See if I am suitable.'

'Of course you are suitable!' Bedelia said sharply. 'It is a formality. And I dare say he was pleased to get out of the city and visit us for a day or two. Cities are so . . . grubby when it snows.'

'It isn't snowing,' he pointed out.

She ignored him. 'At least his visit was not marred by tragedy.'

'Or anything else,' Clara added.

'I think it will snow,' Agnes offered, glancing towards the curtained windows. 'The wind has changed and the clouds were very heavy before sunset.'

Mariah was delighted. Snow might mean she could not leave tomorrow, if it were sufficiently deep. 'Oh dear,' she said with pretended anxiety. 'I did not notice. I do hope I am not imposing on you?'

'Not in the slightest,' Bedelia assured her. 'You say you were a friend of Maude's, even on so short an acquaintance. How could you not be welcome?'

'Of course,' Agnes agreed again, echoing Bedelia. 'You said Maude spoke to you a great deal? We saw her so little, perhaps it would not be too distressing if we were to ask you what she told you of her . . . travels?' She looked hastily at Bedelia. 'That is . . . if it is seemly to discuss! I do not wish to embarrass you in any way at all.'

What on earth was Agnes imagining? Orgies around the campfire?

'Perhaps . . . another time,' Arthur said shakily, his voice hoarse. 'If indeed it does snow, you may be here with us long enough to . . .' He trailed off.

'Quite,' Bedelia agreed, without looking at him.

Zachary apologised. 'We are all overwrought,' he

explained. 'This is so unexpected. We hardly know how to . . . believe it.'

'We had no idea at all that she was ill,' Randolph spoke for the first time since Mariah had come into the room. 'She seemed so . . . so very alive . . . indestructible.'

'You no more than met her, my dear,' Bedelia said coolly.

Mariah turned to her in surprise.

'Maude left before my son was born,' Bedelia explained, as if an intrusive question had been asked. 'I think you do not really understand what an . . . an extraordinary woman she was.' Her use of the word 'extraordinary' covered a multitude of possibilities, most of them unpleasant.

Mariah did not reply. She must detect! The room was stiff with emotion. Grief, envy, anger, above all fear. Did she scent the odour of scandal? For heaven's sake, she was not achieving much! She had no proof that the cause of Maude's death had been murder, only a certainty in her own suspicious mind.

'No,' she said softly. 'Of course I didn't know how extraordinary she was. I spoke with her and listened to her memories and feelings, so very intense, a woman of remarkable observation and understanding. But as you say, it was only a day. I have no right to speak as if I knew her as you must have, who grew up with her.' She let the irony of the forty-year gap hang in the air. 'I imagine when she was abroad she wrote wonderful letters?'

There was an uncomfortable silence, eloquent in itself. So

Maude had not written to them in the passionate and lyrical way she had spoken at St Mary. Or she had, and for some reason they chose to ignore it.

Mariah ploughed on, determined to stir up something that might be of meaning. 'She had travelled as very few people – men or women – can have done. A collection of her letters would be of interest to many who do not have such opportunities. Or such remarkable courage. It would be a fitting monument to her, do you not think?'

Agnes drew in her breath with a gasp, and looked at Bedelia. She seemed helpless to answer without her approval. A lifetime habit forged in childhood? Perhaps forged was the right word; it seemed to fetter her like iron. It made Mariah furious, with Agnes and with herself. It was a coward's way, and she knew cowardice intimately, as one knows one's own face in the glass.

Clara turned to her husband, then her mother-in-law, expecting some response.

But it was Arthur who answered.

'Yes it would,' he agreed.

'Arthur!' Bedelia said crisply. 'I am sure Mrs Ellison means well, but she really has no idea of the extent or the nature of Maude's . . . travels, or the unsuitability of making them public.'

'Have you?' Arthur asked, his dark brows raised.

'I beg your pardon?' Bedelia said coolly.

'Have you any idea of Maude's travels?' he repeated. 'I

asked you if she wrote, and you said that she didn't.' He did not accuse her of lying, but the inevitability of the conclusion was heavy in the air. She sat pale-faced, tight-lipped.

It was Clara who broke the silence. 'Do you think it will still be acceptable for us to have the Matlocks and the Willowbrooks to dine with us on Christmas Eve, Mama-in-law? Or to go to the Watch Night service at Snargate? Or would people think us callous?'

'I don't suppose we can,' Agnes said sadly. 'I was looking forward to it too, my dear.' She looked at Clara, not at Zachary, who had drawn in his breath to say something.

'Death does not alter Christmas,' Bedelia responded after a moment's thought. 'In fact, Christmas is the very time when it means least. It is the season in which we celebrate the knowledge of eternity, and the mercy of God. Of course we shall go to the Watch Night service in Snargate, and show a bond of courage and faith, and solidarity as a family. Don't you think so, my dear?' She looked at Arthur again, as if the previous conversation had never taken place.

'It would seem very appropriate,' he answered to the room in general, no discernible emotion in his voice.

'Oh, I'm so glad,' Agnes responded, smiling. 'And we have so much to be grateful for, it seems only right.'

Mariah thought it an odd remark. For what were they so grateful, just now? The fact that Lord Woollard had considered Arthur suitable for a peerage? Could that matter in the slightest, compared with the death of a sister? Of course it could! Maude had not been home for forty years, and they had considered her absent permanently. She had chosen to return at a highly inconvenient time, otherwise they would not have dispatched her to stay with Joshua and Caroline. Was there really some family scandal she might speak of, and ruin such a high ambition?

Any further speculation on that subject was interrupted by the announcement of dinner.

The meal was excellent, and richer than anything Caroline had offered.

Conversation at the table centred on other arrangements for Christmas, and how they might be affected either by Maude's death, or the weather. They skirted around the issue of a funeral, and when or where it should be conducted, but it hung in the air unsaid, like a coldness, as if someone had left a door open.

Mariah stopped listening to the words and concentrated instead upon the intonation of voices, the ease or tension in hands, and above all the expression in a face when the person imagined they were unnoticed.

Clara appeared relieved, as if an anxiety had passed. Perhaps the visit of Lord Woollard had made her nervous. She might be less confident than she appeared. Had she been socially clumsy or otherwise unacceptable? Since her husband was the only heir, that would have been a serious problem. Perhaps she came from a more ordinary background than the rest of the family and had previously made errors, or her mother was one of those women ruthlessly ambitious for their daughters, and no achievement was great enough?

Zachary did not say a great deal, and Mariah saw him look at Bedelia more often than she would have expected. There was an admiration in him, a sense of awe. For her beauty? She was certainly far better-looking than poor Agnes. She had a glamour, an air of femininity, mystery, almost power, that confidence gave her. Mariah watched her as well, and in spite of herself.

What was it like to be beautiful? There were not many women so blessed; certainly she had never been so herself, and neither was Agnes – nor had Maude been. Clara was no more than handsome. Luminous, heart-stopping beauty was very rare. Even Bedelia did not have that.

Mariah had seen it once or twice, and one did not forget it. Emily's great-aunt by her first marriage, Lady Vespasia Cumming-Gould, possessed it. Even in advanced years it was still there, unmistakable as a familiar song – one note, and the heart brings it all back.

Why did Zachary still watch Bedelia? Ordinary masculine fascination with beauty? Or good manners, because this was her house?

Arthur did not watch her the same way.

Agnes looked at both of them, and seemed to see it also. There was a sadness in her eyes. Was it an awareness that she could never compete? Perhaps that was the sense of failure Mariah detected, and understood. She knew it well:

a plain face; no magic in the eyes or the voice; above all, the knowledge of not being loved.

Envy? Even hate, over the years? Why? Simply beauty? Could it matter so much? Very few women were more than pleasing in their youth, and perhaps gained a little sense of style, or even better, wit, in their maturity. And Agnes had not been left on the shelf. But sisters did compete. It was inevitable. Was money also involved, and now a peerage too?

The conversation continued around her, concern for those who would be alone over the Christmas period and possibly in need, those whose health was poor, anyone to whom they could or should give a small gift. Would the weather deteriorate?

'Do you often get shut in by the snow?' Mariah enquired with interest. 'It must be a rather frightening experience.'

'Not at all,' Zachary assured her. 'We will be quite safe. We have food and fuel, and it will not be for more than a day or two. But please don't concern yourself. If it happens at all, it will be in January and February. You know the old saying: "As the days get longer, the weather gets stronger."' He smiled, transforming his face from its earlier gravity to a surprising warmth.

She smiled back, enjoying the sudden and inexplicable sense of freedom it gave her. 'I have found it very often true,' she agreed. 'And I am sure you are quite wise enough to guard against any possible need. It was rather more such things as someone falling ill that I was thinking of. But I dare say that is a difficulty for all people who live in the wilder and more beautiful country areas.'

She continued being charming. It was like having a new toy. She turned to Bedelia. 'You know, Mrs Harcourt, I would never have seen Romney Marsh as anything more than a very flat coast, rather vulnerable, with a permanent smell of the sea, until I met Miss Barrington. But on our walk I saw how she was aware of so much more! She spoke of the wildflowers in the spring, and the birds. She knew the names of a great many of them, you know, and their habits. The water birds especially.' She was inventing at least part of this as she was going along. It was exhilarating. The surprised and anxious faces around her increased her sense of adventure. She drew in her breath and went on, 'I had never realised before how perfectly everything fits into its own place in the scheme of things.'

'Really?' Bedelia said, her voice almost expressionless. 'It is an interest she had developed recently. In fact since she left England altogether. She must have gained it from reading. She certainly never saw them in life.'

'She did not go walking a great deal?' Mariah asked innocently.

'She was here for only a matter of hours,' Bedelia informed her. 'She did not have time to go out at all. Surely she told you that she arrived without giving us any prior warning, and we were thus unable to accommodate her. Do you imagine we would have asked Joshua Fielding to offer his hospitality were it possible for us to do so ourselves?'

So she was correct! Maude had been given the single dose of peppermint water by someone in the house. She must think very rapidly. Better to retreat than to cause an argument, much as the words stuck in her mouth. Was it better to be considered a fool and of no danger at all, or as a highly knowledgeable woman who needed to be watched? She must decide immediately. She could not be both, and time was short.

Bedelia was waiting. They were all looking at Mariah. A brilliant idea flashed into her mind. She could be both apparently stupid, and extremely clever – if she affected to be a little deaf!

She drew in breath to say so, and apologise for it. Then just before she did, she had another thought of infinitely greater clarity. If she were to claim to be deaf then any evidence she gained could later be denied!

She smothered her pride, a thing she had never done before, except on that unmentionable occasion when her own past had loomed up like a corpse out of the river. But if she had survived that, then nothing this family could do to her would ever make a dent in her inner steel.

'You are quite right,' she said meekly. 'I had forgotten she had been away so very long. If she had no interest before, then it must have been acquired entirely by reading. Perhaps she was homesick for the wide skies, the salt wind and the sound of the sea?'

There was a flash of victory in Bedelia's eyes, a knowledge

of her own power. Mariah felt it as keenly as if it had been a charge of electricity between them such as one is pricked by at times if one touches certain metals when the air is very dry. She had read that predatory animals scented blood in the same way, and it gave her a shiver of fear and intense knowledge of vulnerability, which made life suddenly both sweet and fragile.

Was that what Agnes had known all her life? Or was she being fanciful? What about Maude? Was she crushed too? Was that really why she had left England, and everything familiar that she unquestionably loved, and gone to all kinds of ancient, barbaric, and splendid other lands, where she neither knew anyone nor was known? A desperate escape?

Perhaps, Mariah reflected, there was very much more here, beneath the surface, than she had dreamed, even when she had stood in the bedroom beside Maude's dead body this morning.

Bedelia was smiling. 'Perhaps she was,' she agreed aloud. 'But she could have chosen to live by the sea if she had wished to. Poor Maude had very little sense of how to make decisions, even the right ones. It is most unfortunate.'

'We were hoping to go out far more, later, when she returned . . .' Agnes glanced at Bedelia, 'in the New Year . . . or . . . or whenever we were certain . . .' She trailed off, knowing that somehow she had put her foot in it.

Mariah stared at her, willing her to explain.

Bedelia sighed impatiently. 'Agnes, dear, you really do let

your tongue run away with you!' She turned to Mariah in exasperation. 'You had better know the truth, Mrs Ellison, or you will feel that we are a cruel family. And it is not so at all. Maude was our middle sister, and she was always unruly, the one who had to draw attention to herself by being different. It happens in families at times. The eldest have attention because they are first, the youngest because they are the babies, the middle ones feel left out, and they show off, to use a common term.'

'Maude was not a show-off,' Arthur corrected her. 'She was an enthusiast. Whatever she did, it was with a whole heart. There was nothing affected or contrived in her.'

Bedelia did not look away from Mariah. 'My husband is a man of extraordinarily generous spirit. It is his work for the less fortunate for which Her Majesty is offering him a peerage. I am immensely proud of him, because it is from the noblest of reasons, nothing tawdry like finance, or political support.' She smiled patiently. 'But occasionally his judgement is rather more kind than accurate. It was apparent as soon as she arrived that Maude had travelled in places where manners and customs are quite different from ours. I'm afraid that even her language was not such that we could subject our other guests to her . . . her more colourful behaviour. We knew that Joshua, being on the stage, might be more tolerant of eccentricity. Of course, we could not know that you also would be staying with him, and if Maude has shocked you or made you uncomfortable, then we are guilty of having caused that, and on behalf of all of us, I apologise. Our inconsideration in that regard is what has been disturbing Agnes.'

Agnes smiled, but there were tears in her eyes.

'I see.' Mariah tried to imagine Maude as an embarrassment so severe as to be intolerable. She did not know Lord Woollard. Perhaps he was insufferably pompous. There certainly were people so consumed by their own emotional inadequacy and imagined virtue as to take offence at the slightest thing. And the Maude she had met would find a certain delight in puncturing the absurd, the self-important and, above all, the false. It would be a scene to be avoided. If Arthur Harcourt had done as much for others as Bedelia said, then he was deserving of recognition and, more importantly, the added power to do more good that such an accolade would offer him.

'I'm sure you do,' Bedelia said gently.

'All families seem to have their difficult members,' Zachary added ruefully.

Mariah had an unpleasant feeling that in her family it was she herself. Although Caroline was now giving her some competition, marrying an actor so much younger than herself! And there was Charlotte, of course, and her policeman!

A short while later the ladies retired to the withdrawing room and she learned little more of interest. She considered enquiring after people's health, but could think of no way of approaching the subject without being catastrophically obvious. She was extremely tired. It had been one of the longest days of her life, beginning with tragedy and horror, and ending with mystery, and the growing certainty in her mind that someone in this house had poisoned Maude's medicine. Exactly how it had been achieved, and with what, she had yet to ascertain. Even more important to her was why. Maude had been successfully sent to stay with Joshua. Lord Woollard had been and gone. What was the element so precious, or so terrible, that it was worth murder?

She excused herself, thanked her hosts again for their hospitality and went up to her room. Please heaven it would snow tonight, or in some other way make it impossible for her to leave. There was so much she had to learn. This detection matter was more difficult than she had supposed, and against her will she was being drawn into other people's lives. She cared about Maude, there was no use denying that any more. She disliked Bedelia and had felt the strength of her power. She was sorry for Agnes without knowing why. Arthur intrigued her. In spite of all that was said about him, his success and his goodness to others, she felt an unnamed emotion that disturbed her. It did not fit in.

Randolph and Clara were still too undefined, except that Clara had great social ambitions. Could that possibly be enough to inspire murder?

It was all swirling around in her head as she put on the housekeeper's nightgown and climbed into the bed, intending to weigh it all more carefully, and instead fell asleep almost immediately.

The following morning Mariah slept in, and was embarrassed to waken with the chambermaid standing at the foot of the bed with tea on a tray, and an enquiry what she would care for, for breakfast.

Would two lightly boiled eggs and some toast be possible?

Indeed it would, with the greatest pleasure.

After enjoying it, in spite of the circumstances and the thoughts that occupied her mind, she rose and washed. She dressed in the housekeeper's other black gown, again with the chambermaid's assistance, and found she rather enjoyed talking to her. Then she made her way downstairs.

She met Agnes in the hall. She was wearing outdoor clothes and apparently about to leave.

'Good morning, Mrs Ellison,' she said hastily. 'I do hope you slept well? Such a distressing time for you. I hope you were comfortable? And warm enough?'

'I have never been more comfortable,' Mariah replied with honesty. 'You are most generous. I do not believe I stirred all night. Are you about to go out?'

'Yes. I have a few jars of jam and chutney to take to various friends. Nearby villages, you know? I am afraid the weather does not look promising.'

Mariah had another burst of illumination, of double worth. She could catch Agnes alone, unguarded by Bedelia, and, if the weather did not oblige by snowing them in, she could affect to have caught a slight chill to prevent her returning to St Mary in the Marsh tomorrow, or worse, this afternoon.

'May I come with you?' she asked eagerly. 'I am not here beyond this brief Christmas period, and I would so love to see a little of the outside. It is quite unlike London. So much wider . . . and cleaner. The city always seems grubby when the snow has been trodden, and everything is stained with smoke from so many chimney fires.'

'But of course!' Agnes said with pleasure. 'It would be most agreeable to have your company. But it will be cold. You must wear your cape, and I will have another travelling rug brought for you.'

Mariah thanked her sincerely, and ten minutes later they were sitting side by side in the pony trap driven by a young footman. It was, as Agnes had warned, extremely cold. The wind had the kiss of ice on it. Clouds streamed in from the seaward side and the marsh grasses bent and rippled as if passed over by an unseen hand.

The trap was well sprung and the pony inexplicably enthusiastic, but it was still not the most comfortable ride. They left the village of Snave and moved quite quickly in what Mariah presumed to be a westerly direction, and slightly south. It was all a matter of judging the wind and the smell of the sea. Agnes began by companionably telling her something about the village of Snargate and its inhabitants, and then explaining that from Snargate they would continue to

Appledore. Then if there were time, to the Isle of Oxney as well, which, of course, was not an island at all, simply a rise from the flat land of the coast. However, if there were floods, then it would live up to its name.

Mariah thought that possibly the history of these ancient villages might be quite interesting, but at present it was the history of the Barrington sisters that demanded her entire attention. She must direct Agnes to it, and not waste precious time, of which there was far too little as it was.

'You speak of the land so knowledgably.' She began with flattery. It always worked. 'Your family has its roots here? You belong here?' People always wanted to belong. No one wished to be a stranger, as Maude must have been all her adult life.

'Oh, yes,' Agnes said warmly. 'My great-great-grand-father inherited the house and added to it a hundred and fifty years ago. It is Bedelia's, of course. We had no brothers, unfortunately. And then it will be Randolph's. But then it would have been his anyway, because I have no sons either.' She turned her face forwards so Mariah could see no more than a fleeting moment of her expression, and the moisture in her eyes could have been from the east wind. It was certainly cold enough.

'You are fortunate to have sisters,' Mariah told her. 'I grew up with only brothers, and they were a great deal older than I. Too much so to be my friends,' Mariah lied again.

'I'm sorry.' There was no expression in Agnes's face, no lift of memory that made her smile.

'You must have Christmas memories, and traditions in the family?' Mariah looked at the baskets of jars, the tops covered with dainty cloth and tied with ribbons. 'You do those so very well.' More flattery, even if true.

'We always have,' Agnes answered, still no lift in her voice.

Mariah continued to probe, and finally drew a few more specific answers. In heaven's name, it was hard work! Did Pitt always have such a struggle? It was worse than pulling out teeth. But she was determined. Justice might depend upon this.

'I imagine you all did this together, when you were girls,' she said with what she knew was tactlessness. 'Or perhaps you were courting? I can think of nothing more romantic.' Had she gone too far?

'Zachary did, with Bedelia,' Agnes replied. 'It was this season, and terribly cold. Several of the streams froze that year. I remember it.' She remained looking forward, her expression bleak as the wind pulled strands of her hair loose and whipped them across her face.

Mariah was momentarily lost. Zachary was Agnes's husband. She would dearly like to let this go. She heard pain in Agnes's voice, and old griefs were none of her affair. But Maude was dead. She could not feel the sting of salt in the air or see the wild flight of seabirds skittering down the wind and whirling back up again, high and wide, wheeling far out over the land.

'Mrs Harcourt is very beautiful, even now,' she tested the verbal knife. 'She must have been quite breathtaking then. I have a distant relative who was like that.'

'Yes.' Agnes's hands were tight on the reins, the leather of her gloves strained. 'Half the young men in the county were in love with her.'

'And she chose Mr Harcourt?' It was a stupid question, and probably entirely irrelevant to Maude's death, but Mariah had nothing better to pursue.

'Yes.' For a moment it seemed as if Agnes was going to say no more. Then she drew in her breath, wanting to speak after all. 'Although it was not so simple as that.'

'Really? I suppose things seldom are,' Mariah said sympathetically. 'And even less often are they what they seem to be on the surface. People make very hasty judgements, sometimes.'

'They are the easiest,' Agnes agreed. She negotiated a sharp turn in the lane and Mariah saw the village of Snargate ahead. This was proving very difficult indeed. They were almost at the village green. The inn, the church with ancient yew trees and graveyard, and the lich-gate covered with the bare vines of honeysuckle lay beyond.

They made their first delivery of Christmas fare, and the second, and then left Snargate, bound the short distance to Appledore.

'I suppose there is always speculation where there are sisters, and one is as beautiful as Bedelia,' Mariah said as soon as they were on the way again, blankets carefully tucked around shivering knees. The sky cleared a little and banners of blue appeared bright between the clouds.

As if deliberately hurting herself, Agnes told the story. 'Maude didn't know about it, not really. She was away that Christmas. Aunt Josephine was ill and alone, and Maude went to look after her. Zachary was courting Bedelia. He was so in love with her. They went everywhere together, to the balls and the dinners and the theatre in Dover, even through the snow. That was when the Queen was young and happy, and Prince Albert was so dashing. We saw drawings of them in the newspapers. It was before the Crimean War. I expect you remember?'

'I do.' It had been a nightmare time. Her own husband had been alive, charming, persuasive, privately brutal, demanding things no decent woman ever imagined. She could still taste the wool of the carpet in her mouth and remember his weight on top of her, forcing her down. In public it had been all contentment, the glamour of endless crinoline skirts on a figure unrecognisable now in her too ample waist and hips. And at home a hell she could not think of without a hot shame making her feel sick. How could she, of all people, criticise anyone's cowardice? It stirred in her rage and pity, and a hunger to avenge it so sharp she could taste it in her mouth. The bitter wind was almost a comfort.

But Agnes was lost in her own passions and did not even glance to see if her companion were with her mentally. 'Then

Arthur Harcourt arrived,' she went on. 'I think it was early March. The beginning of spring. The days were getting longer and everything was coming into bud. Arthur was not only handsome but charming and funny and kind. He could make us all laugh so hard we were embarrassed to be caught at it. One did not enjoy things so openly then. It was thought to be unladylike. He didn't care. And he could dance like an angel. Everything seemed worth doing when he was with us.'

Mariah thought she could guess the rest. Bedelia fell out of love with Zachary and in love with Arthur, who was a far better catch. Poor Zachary was cast aside, and in time took second best, the duller, plainer Agnes. And lacking the heart or the belief in herself to fight it, Agnes accepted.

Without thinking, Mariah reached across and put her hand on Agnes's where it rested above the edge of the rug, holding the reins tightly. She did not say anything. It was a silent understanding, a pity without words.

For a few moments they rode through the lanes towards Appledore in silence.

Then suddenly Agnes spoke again. 'Of course we thought then that Bedelia and Arthur would marry. It seemed inevitable.'

'Yes, it would,' Mariah agreed.

'But Aunt Josephine died, and Maude came back home. Everything changed,' Agnes said.

'Indeed?' Mariah had almost forgotten about Maude. 'How?'

'Arthur and Maude just . . .' Agnes gave a tiny shrug, 'just seemed to . . . to fall so in love it was as if Bedelia ceased to exist. It didn't seem like a flirtation. Bedelia was . . . unable to believe it at first. I mean Maude, of all people. Goodness knows what she told him!'

'Told him?' Mariah said before she could stop herself.

'Well, she must have told him something terrible about Bedelia to have caused him to abandon her like that! And, of course, untrue. Jealousy is . . . a very unkind thing. It eats the heart out of you, if you allow it to.'

'Oh, that is true,' Mariah agreed sincerely. 'It can be an instant passion, or a slow-growing one, but it is certainly deadly. But it seems as if Arthur saw through it, whatever it was.' She hated saying that because it blamed Maude, and she was far from prepared to do that, but she must keep Agnes telling the story.

'Oh, yes,' Agnes agreed. 'It lasted perhaps a month, then Arthur came to his senses. He realised that he truly loved Bedelia. He broke off the silly business with Maude, and asked Bedelia to marry him. Of course, she forgave him, and accepted.'

'I see.' She did not see at all.

Three sisters, two men. Someone had to have lost. Mariah resented that it should have been Maude. Or had it really been all of them, no one truly finding what they hungered for? 'And Maude?' she said quietly.

'Maude was heartbroken,' Agnes replied, her voice

catching in her throat. She turned away as if there were something on the other side of the pony trap that required her attention, although there was nothing but the grasses and the sea wind and the marsh stretching out to the horizon. 'She simply ran away. God knows where she went, but about a month later we received a postcard from Granada, in the south of Spain. There were only a few words on it. I remember. "Going to Africa. Will probably stay. Maude."'

And Bedelia had said she never wrote again. Was that true? 'Until she returned a few days ago?' Mariah asked aloud.

'That's right.'

'Why did she come back, now, after all these years?'

Agnes shook her head and rubbed her hand over her eyes. 'Perhaps she knew she was dying. Maybe she wanted to be buried here. People do. Want to be buried in the their own land, I mean, their own earth.'

'Did she say anything like that?'

'She did say something about death. I can't recall exactly what it was. But she was sad, that much was clear. I . . . I wish I had listened. My mind was on Lord Woollard's visit, and how anxious we all were that it should go well.' Guilt was heavy in her voice and the misery of her face. 'Arthur really does deserve recognition, you know. And the amount of good he could do with it would be enormous.'

'And you were concerned that Maude's behaviour would be inappropriate?'

Agnes glanced at Mariah, then away again, a mixture of

impatience and shame in her face. 'She had been living in extraordinary places for the last forty years, Mrs Ellison. Places where people eat with their fingers, have no running water, where women do things that . . . I would rather not even think of, let alone speak about.'

'I thought women in the Middle East were rather more modest than we are here in England,' Mariah said thoughtfully. 'At least that was the impression I gained from Maude. They keep to their own apartments and don't speak to men other than those in their own families. Their clothing is certainly most decorous.'

Agnes was frowning. 'But Maude went unaccompanied, wandering around like a . . . like a man!' she exclaimed. 'Who knows what happened to her? Her taste is highly questionable. Even her virtue, I'm afraid.'

'I beg your pardon?' Mariah said in angry disbelief, then realised she had gone too far. She must find an escape very quickly. 'I'm so sorry,' she apologised, the words all but choking her. 'I felt so close to Maude because she confided in me, and I in her, that I am more offended than I have any right to be at the thought that someone who did not know her at all should question her virtue. It is quite unreasonable, and even impertinent of me. Please forgive me. She was your sister, not mine, and it is your right to defend her. I did not mean to presume.' She watched Agnes's face intently, as if she were eager for pardon. She was actually extremely eager to see Agnes's reaction.

Agnes's hands froze on the reins and she stared ahead, even though they were now very close to the village of Appledore and she should have been slowing the pony.

'It is not presumptuous,' she said, her face scarlet. Then she stopped again, still uncertain. 'I'm sure you meant it only kindly. Perhaps we live too much in the past. Imagine too much.'

'About Maude?' Mariah had to ask. She was overwhelmingly aware of the misery in Agnes, and the knowledge that she would always be second choice. She was sorry for it – she even understood it – but it did not excuse lies, or answer justice now. They were passing the village church and she saw the festive wreaths on doors, and a group of children ran past them shouting greetings. What happens to people that they become bitter, and why do we not turn to each other, and help, Mariah wondered. We all walk a common path from cradle to grave, just stumble over different stones in it, trip in different holes, or drown in different puddles.

Agnes had not answered her.

'I understand,' Mariah said impulsively. 'You had old memories of Maude once taking Arthur's affection, and you were afraid she would say or do something outrageous now. Perhaps even spoil Arthur's chances of receiving a peerage. So you made sure she could not be in the house when Lord Woollard was here. And now that she has died, you feel guilty, and of course it is too late to do anything about it.'

Agnes turned to face her, eyes wide and hurt. She said

nothing, but acknowledgement was as clear in her as if she had admitted it in so many words.

They delivered the jam and chutney in Appledore and went on to the Isle of Oxney. The rising wind was cruelly cold. The horizon was blurred with gathering clouds and there was a smell of snow in the air. Perhaps it would not be necessary for Mariah to feign a chill after all. Although how deep the snow would have to be to make travel inadvisable she did not know. St Mary in the Marsh was only five miles away, not even an hour's journey. Maybe a few sneezes and a complaint of a sore throat would be better. She had barely scratched the surface of what there was to detect. There were emotions, old loves and jealousies, old wrongs, but what had caused them to erupt now? Pitt had said that there was always a reason why violence occurred at a particular time, some event that sparked the final act.

Why had Maude come home? Why not before, in all the forty years of her exile? Or next year? Why at Christmas, not summer, when the weather would be infinitely more agreeable? Whose death was it she had been referring to? Surely not her own?

Deliberately on the ride back to Snave Mariah spoke only of Christmas arrangements with Agnes. What to eat? Goose, naturally, plenty of vegetables roasted, boiled, baked and with added sauces. And after, there would be a Christmas pudding, rich with dried fruit and covered with brandied butter, and flamed at the time of serving. And with cream.

But before that there were literally dozens of other things to think of and prepare: cakes, pastries, mince pies, sweets, gingerbread and all manner of drinks, both with alcohol and without. And naturally a wealth of decoration: wreaths and boughs, garlands, golden angels, coloured bows, flowers made of silk and ribbon, pine cones painted with gold, little dolls to be given afterwards to the poor of the village. There were presents to be made: skittles painted as wooden soldiers, pin cushions, ornaments hand made and decorated with lace and beads and coloured braid. The hours of work could hardly be counted. They spoke of them together, and remembered about their own childhood Christmases, before the advent of cards and trees and such modern ideas that so much added to the general happiness.

After luncheon Mariah took a brief walk in the garden between showers. She needed time alone to think. Detection required order in the mind. There were facts to be considered and weighed.

There was little to see beyond a well-tended neatness and very obvious architectural grace and skill. There were arbours, gravel walks, herbaceous borders carefully weeded, perennials cleared of dead foliage, a flight of steps curved up to a pergola covered with the skeletons of roses, and finally a less formal woodland overlooking the open marsh.

It was very wet underfoot, and rather muddy. The long grasses soaked the hem of her skirt, but it was inevitable. In

spring this would be beautiful with flowers: snowdrops, prim-
roses in all likelihood, wood anemones, certainly bluebells,
wild daisies, campion. Perhaps narcissi with their piercingly
sweet scent. She saw two or three crowns of foxglove leaves.
She loved their elegant spires in purples or white. One of
them looked a little ragged, as if an animal had cropped it.
Except that no animal would eat foxglove – it was poisonous.
Creatures always seemed to know. It slowed the heart. It was
used by doctors for people whose hearts raced. Digitalis. She
froze. Raced . . . slowed. Stopped!

Was that it? The answer she was searching for? She bent
and looked at the leaves again. There was no earthly way of
proving it, but she was perfectly sure someone had picked
two or three leaves. The broken ends were visible.

She stood up again slowly. How could she find out who?
It must have been the day Maude was here. Had it been wet
or dry? Never dry in winter in this wood, but if freezing then
the ice would prevent anyone getting as wet as she was now,
or as muddy.

The day before Joshua had received Bedelia's letter. Think!
Windy, the noise of it howling in the eaves was clear in her
mind. It had irritated her unbearably. And relatively mild.
Who had come in with muddy boots, a dress soaked at the
hems? A lady's maid would know. But how to ask her?

Mariah turned and walked briskly back into the house, and
went to find Mrs Ward.

'I'm so sorry,' she apologised profusely; startled that she

meant it without any pretence at all. 'I went walking in the garden and became distracted with the beauty of it.'

'It is lovely, isn't it?' Mrs Ward agreed. 'That's Mrs Harcourt's skill. Mrs Sullivan can paint a picture of a flower that's both lovely and correct, but it's Mrs Harcourt who plans the garden itself.'

'What a gift,' Mariah said. 'And one from which we all benefit. But I am afraid that I have thoroughly muddied both my boots, and the hem of your dress. It was deeply careless of me, and I regret it now.'

'Oh, don't worry! It happens all the time!' Mrs Ward dismissed it. 'Your own dress is quite clean and dry, and Nora can clean this again in no time.'

'I'm sure it doesn't happen to everybody,' Mariah told her. 'I cannot imagine Mrs Harcourt being so inelegant, or so thoughtless. You cannot name me the last time she did this!'

Mrs Ward smiled. 'Certainly I can! The very day Miss Maude came home. Went looking for some nice branches to add to the flowers in the hall. Woodland branches can be most graceful in a vase. Please don't think of it, Mrs Ellison.'

'Really?' Mariah's heart was racing. So it was Bedelia. But she should be certain. 'I expect she and Mr Harcourt were in quite a state, with Lord Woollard expected as well.'

'Certainly. She also went out on an errand and came back as muddy as you like. Poor Nora was beside herself. Then Mrs Sullivan the day after. At least I think it was. I'll find Nora and send her up to you.'

'Thank you. You are most considerate.' Mariah left with her mind whirling. So they were all outside. Who had boiled up the leaves? Where? How could she find that out? Perhaps they were simply crushed and steeped, as one makes a cup of tea! That could have been any of them. She must think more – pay attention. And be careful!

In the afternoon Mariah offered to help Bedelia in some of the last-minute preparations. Of course, Cook would see to the meal itself, and most of the other things that required the use of the kitchen. But there was still much sewing to be done, lavender bags that were not finished, ornamental roses to be made and definitely more decorations for the great tree in the hall.

'I could have sworn that we had more than this last year!' Bedelia said, looking at it with dismay. 'It seems almost bare, don't you think, Mrs Ellison?'

Mariah regarded the huge tree, its dark green needles still fresh and scented with earth and pine. It was liberally decorated with ribbons and ornaments, and there was a handsome pile of parcels beneath, and smaller ones with lace and flowers on hanging from the branches. It was far from bare, but certainly there were places where more could be hung. It was important that she make herself necessary.

'It is very handsome,' she answered judiciously. 'But you are quite right, of course. There are still one or two places to be filled in. I am sure it would not be difficult to find the materials to make a couple of dozen more ornaments. One needs only a child's ball, perhaps two of different sizes would be even better, paste, and as many different colours of paper as possible, beads, dried flowers, ribbon, lace, whatever else can be spared that is pretty. Sometimes an old gown can provide an amazing variety of bits and pieces. It's not difficult to make tiny dolls, or angels.' She had rather run away with herself, but it was all in the growingly desperate cause of detection. Very definite ideas were crystallising in her mind, but she needed more time!

Christmas was supposed to be a time of forgiveness, but surely there could be no healing without honour, no real peace without change of heart? And no change without truth.

'It is not a lack of materials,' Bedelia told her. 'I have not the time, and I doubt the maids have the skill.'

'I should be happy to help you, if I may?' Mariah offered. She had not been so courteous in years, and in spite of her amusement at herself, she was rather enjoying it. It was like a step outside her own life, a curious freedom from the expectations of others, or the chains of past failure. 'I should be delighted to contribute something to such a glorious tree,' she continued eagerly. 'And also a sort of family tradition. The Barringtons have been in this village for so many generations there are bound to be scores of people who will call in to wish you season's greetings and share your hospitality.' That was certain. Tradesmen always paid their respects this time of year and partook of mince pies, candied fruit and nuts, and, of course, a cup of punch.

Bedelia accepted, and half an hour later they were sitting in the sewing room at opposite sides of the table, cannibalising an old evening gown, cutting off beads, braid, fine silk and velvet pieces, and the paler ribbons and lace from two old petticoats that had also been found.

'There is too much dark red,' Bedelia said critically. 'All of the silk and velvet is the same shade.'

'That is true,' Mariah agreed. 'What we really need is something else bright in a completely different tone.' She looked at Bedelia with a frown. 'I have a very daring idea. Perhaps you would find it offensive, but I have to ask. If it grieves you, I apologise in advance.'

'Good gracious!' Bedelia was intrigued. 'I am not easily shocked. What is this idea?'

'Maude said that she travelled in many strange and exotic places.'

A faint distaste flashed in Bedelia's eyes but she masked it. 'Is that helpful?'

'No doubt she wore some . . . strange clothes,' Mariah said tentatively. 'Possibly of colours we would not choose.'

Bedelia understood instantly and her face lit with pleasure.

'Oh! But of course! How clever of you. Yes, certainly, some of them might be cut up for the most excellent Christmas ornaments.'

Mariah felt a chill at the thought of cutting up any of Maude's clothes, things she had worn in the places so far from home that she had obviously loved. She might have stood in the sunset in some Persian garden and smelled the perfume of strange trees and the wind off the desert, and looked up to unimaginable stars. Or perhaps there would be scarves of silk she had bought at a noisy, multitudinous bazaar in Marrakesh, or some such city. They should all be treated with tenderness, folded to keep in the odour of spices and strange fruit, oils and leathers and the smoke from the camp-fires.

'You are so clever, Mrs Ellison,' Bedelia was saying. 'Of course most of her things are here and we have only to unpack them. And it is unlikely that any of them are things that anyone else would wear. I really do not care to offer them, even to the poor. It would be . . .'

'Disrespectful,' Mariah filled in, meaning it, and enjoying forcing Bedelia to agree. She hated herself for doing it, but truth required some strange sacrifices. 'This way they will be totally anonymous, and give pleasure for years to come.' Forgive me, Maude, she thought to herself. Detection is not easy, and I refuse to fail. She stood up. 'I suppose we should begin. See what we can find.' That was crass. She had not been invited to look into Maude's effects, but she was most curious to see if there was anything helpful. No one else who knew that she had been murdered would ever have such an opportunity.

If Bedelia were offended she did not show it.

Upstairs in the boxroom, where the luggage had been stored, they set about opening the two trunks Maude had brought back with her. Mariah found herself with the one packed with ordinary blouses and skirts, underwear and sensible, rather scuffed boots. They were of moderate quality linen, cotton and some of raw, unbleached wool. She wondered in what marvellous places Maude had worn these. What had she seen, what emotions of joy, pain or loneliness had she felt? Had she longed for home, or had she been at home wherever she was, with friends, even people who loved her?

She glanced across at Bedelia and studied her face as she pulled out a length of silk striped in purples, scarlets, crimsons, and tawny golds mingled with a hot pink. She drew in her breath sharply. At first it seemed to be pleasure, excitement, even a kind of longing. Then her mouth hardened and there was hurt in her eyes.

'Good heavens above!' she said sharply. 'What on earth could she have worn this for? Whatever is it?' She shook it out until it billowed and appeared to be a sheet with very little distinctive shape. 'One can only hope it was a gift, and not something she purchased for herself. No woman could wear such a thing, even at twenty, never mind at Maude's age! She would have looked like something out of the circus!' She started to laugh, then stopped abruptly. 'A very good thing we looked at this first, Mrs Ellison. If the servants had seen it we should be the talk of the village.'

Mariah felt her fury flare up and if she had dared she would have lashed out verbally in Maude's defence. But there were bigger considerations, and with intense difficulty she choked back the words. She forced herself to look as close to good-natured as she could manage, which effort cost her dearly. 'Instead they will be talking about the gorgeous and perfectly unique ornaments on your tree,' she said sweetly. 'And you will be able to say that they are a remembrance of your sister.'

Bedelia sat rigid, her eyes unmoving, her face set. It could have been grief, or the complexity and hurt of any memory, including anger that would never now be redeemed, or regret for forgiveness too late. Or even debts uncollected. The only thing Mariah was certain of was that the emotion was deep, and that it brought no ease or pleasure.

They took the silks downstairs and Bedelia cut into them with large fabric shears. Bright clouds like desert sunsets drifted across the table and on to the floor. Mariah picked them up and began to work on the papier-mâché and paste to make the basic balls before they should be covered in the bright gauze. After that they would stitch little dolls to dress in the gold and bronze and white with pearls. She smiled at the prospect. It was fun to create beauty.

But she was not here to enjoy herself. This silk in her hands had been a wonderful, wild, garish robe that Maude had worn on the hot roads of Arabia, or somewhere like it.

'I imagine Maude must have known some very different people,' she said thoughtfully. 'They would seem odd to us, perhaps even frightening.' She allowed the lamplight to fall on the purple silk and the brazen red. 'I cannot imagine wearing these colours together.'

'Nor could anyone else outside a fairground!' Bedelia responded. 'You see why we could not have her here when Lord Woollard stayed. We allowed him the courtesy of not shocking or embarrassing him.'

'Is he a man of small experience?' Mariah enquired with as much innocence as she could contrive.

'Of discreet taste and excellent family,' Bedelia said coolly. 'His wife, whom I have met, is the sister of one of Her Majesty's ladies-in-waiting. An excellent person.'

Perhaps even a week ago Mariah would have been impressed. Now all she could think of was Maude's Persian garden with the small owls in the dusk.

There was a knock on the door and Agnes came in. A brief conversation followed about parties, games to be played, especially Blind Man's Buff, and, of course, refreshments.

'We must remember some lemon curd tarts for Mrs Hethersett,' Agnes reminded her. 'She is always so fond of them.'

'She will have to make her own,' Bedelia responded. 'She will not be coming.'

'Oh dear! Is she unwell again?' Agnes asked sympathetically.

'She will not be coming because I have not invited her,' Bedelia said tersely. 'She was unforgivably rude.'

'That was over a year ago!' Agnes protested.

'It was,' Bedelia agreed. 'What has that to do with it?'

Agnes did not argue. She admired the rapidly progressing baubles, and returned to the task of organising pies and tarts.

'How very unpleasant,' Mariah sympathised, wondering what on earth Mrs Hethersett could have said that Bedelia still bore a grudge about a year later, and at Christmas, of all times. 'She must have been dreadfully rude to distress you so much.' She nearly added that she could not understand why people should be rude, but that was too big a lie to swallow. She could understand rudeness perfectly, and practise it to the level of an art. It was something she had never previously been ashamed of, but now it was oddly distasteful to her.

'She imagines I will forget,' Bedelia responded. 'But she is quite mistaken, as she will learn.'

Mariah bent to the stitching again, blending the bright colours with less pleasure, and wondered what Maude had done to Bedelia that old memories lingered so long in unforgiveness. After all, Arthur had married Bedelia in the end, and it was Maude who had left home alone.

Why had Maude returned now? Was it possible Mariah was completely mistaken? Had she allowed her bored and lonely imagination to conjure up murder where there was only an unexpected death, and grief that looked like anger? And a proud woman who would not allow another to see that she was bitterly ashamed of having turned away her sister for fear that her behaviour was socially inappropriate, and now regretted it so terribly when it was too late? Was Mariah making a crime out of what was only a tragedy?

Dinner was tense again. As on the first night, there was the palpable undercurrent of emotions that perhaps there always is in families: knowledge of weaknesses, indulgences, things said that would have been better forgotten, only there is always someone who will remind.

Aloud they recalled past Christmases, particularly those when Randolph had been a boy, which necessarily excluded Clara. Mariah studied her face and saw the flicker of hurt in it, and then of arrogance.

The others were enjoying themselves. For once Arthur joined in the laughter and the open affection as Bedelia told a tale of Randolph's surprise at receiving a set of tin soldiers in perfect replica of Wellington's army at Waterloo. It seemed he had refused to come to the table, even for goose. He was so enraptured he could not put his soldiers down. Bedelia had tried to insist, but Arthur had said it was Christmas, and Randolph should do as he pleased.

Mariah found herself smiling also – until she saw the hunger in Zachary's eyes, his look at Bedelia, Agnes's look at him, and remembered that Randolph was the only one among all four of them likely to have a child. He was forty. Clara, strong-willed and ambitious, was a great deal younger. When would they have children? Or might that be another grief waiting in the wings?

She would like to have had more children herself, a

daughter like Charlotte might have made all the difference, or even like Emily. A lot of work, a lot of frustration and disappointment, but who could measure the happiness?

It would be better if she did not think of the past any more. Far better to treasure what you have than grieve over what you have not.

She looked around their faces again. Why does anybody hate someone enough to kill them, with all the risk involved? You don't, if you are sane. You kill to protect, to keep what you have and love: position, power, money, even safety from scandal, the pain of humiliation, or loss, or the terror in loneliness. She could imagine that, except that she had no need to. She had tried once, ludicrously, terrifyingly. She had been kept from disaster only by her own incompetence. Perhaps we were all as fragile, if one found the right passion, the fear that eats at the soul.

She looked at the light from the chandeliers glittering on the silver, the crystal, the white linen, the lilies from the hothouse and the red wine, all the different faces, and wondered if she really wanted to know the answer.

Then she remembered Maude's laughter, and the memories in her eyes as she described the moonlight over the desert. There was no escaping the answer. That would be the ultimate, irredeemable cowardice.

The following day the scullery maid cut her finger so badly she could not use her hand, and the kitchen was in pandemonium. Agnes had been going to take the pony trap to deliver gifts to the vicar's widow in Dymchurch, and now all plans had to be rearranged.

Without a thought for her own competence for such a task, Mariah offered to go in her stead. The stable boy could drive her and she would call, with explanations, upon Mrs Dowson and give her the already wrapped gifts for herself, and one or two other families.

Her offer was accepted, and at ten o'clock they set off, she feeling very pleased with herself. It was a bitter day with clouds piling slate grey on the horizon, and the wind had veered round to come from the north with ice on its edge.

Mariah sat with the rug wrapped tightly around her knees and tucked in under her, hoping profoundly that it would not snow before she returned to Snave, or she might find that the chill she had considered pretending to have could be only too real. She had no desire whatever to spend Christmas in bed with a fever!

And then another thought assailed her, even more unpleasant. What if she discovered beyond doubt who it was that had picked the foxglove leaves and distilled their poison, and could prove it? And that person became aware of the fact! Then it might be a great deal more than a chill that afflicted her. She wondered if it was painful to die of a heart slowing until it stopped altogether. She could feel it bumping in her chest now with fear.

If she died, would anyone miss her enough to be sorry?

Would anyone's world be colder or greyer because she was not in it?

She thought of Maude, alone in the house of strangers who had taken her in out of kindness, or worse, a sense of duty. Or pity? That was even worse again. Had Maude felt obliged to work hard to be charming, hide the rejection she must feel inside in order to win their warmth? Had she even known that Mariah liked her – genuinely liked her?

Now, that was a lie. Her face was hot in spite of the knife-edge wind. She had loathed Maude, even before she arrived, because she would displace her as the centre of attention. She had realised only after Maude was dead how much she had liked her, admired her, found her exciting to listen to, freeing the imagination and awakening dreams. She wished now, with a desire so strong it was like a physical ache, that she had allowed Maude to see that she liked her, and very much so.

They were going towards the sea and she could smell the salt more sharply. Dymchurch was not far from St Mary in the Marsh. She could not return home until she had solved this. It would be a betrayal not only of Maude, but of friendship itself. The length of it was irrelevant, it was the depth that mattered.

She ignored the great ragged skies, clouds streaming across its vastness like the torn banners of an army, spears of ice not far behind. As they drove into the village itself she could hear the roaring of the surf on the shore, and the tower of the church seemed to stand aloft against the racing darkness coming in on the storm.

They pulled up at a small cottage with bare vines covering the arch over the gate and the stable boy announced that they had arrived. He said he would take the parcels in for her, as soon as they had ascertained that Mrs Dowson was at home. Then he would take the pony and trap around to the stable to shelter until Mrs Ellison was ready to leave again. He looked anxiously at the sky, and then smiled, showing gapped teeth.

Mariah thanked him and, with his help, alighted.

Mrs Dowson was at home. She was a lean woman with narrow shoulders and bright eyes. She must have been closer to eighty than seventy, but seemed to be still in excellent health. There was a colour in her cheeks as if she had recently been outside, even in this darkening weather.

Mariah introduced herself.

'My name is Mariah Ellison, Mrs Dowson. Please excuse me for calling unannounced on Mrs Harcourt's behalf, but I am afraid I have accepted their hospitality in the wake of tragedy, and the whole family is bravely making the very best of a hard situation. I offered to come on this errand for her. I feel it is the least I can do.'

'Oh dear. I'm so sorry. Very kind of you, Mrs Ellison.' She looked at Mariah curiously but without apprehension. 'May I offer you tea, and perhaps a mince pie or something of the sort?' She did not ask what the tragedy had been. Was that extreme discretion, or had word somehow come this far already?

'Thank you,' Mariah accepted, wondering if there were a third possibility – that she simply did not care. 'I admit, it is remarkably cold outside. I do not know this area very well. I live in London and am merely visiting, but I find something most pleasing about the sea air, even when there is so very much of it.'

Mrs Dowson smiled. 'It pleases me too,' she agreed, conducting the way into a small but very pretty sitting room. It was low-ceilinged, with furniture covered in floral chintz, and a fire burning in the hearth. She rang the bell, and when the maid came, requested tea and tarts.

'Now, my dear,' she said when they were seated. 'What is the trouble with poor Agnes now? I imagine it is Agnes, is it not?'

How interesting, Mariah thought. Aloud she said, 'I am afraid it is all of them. Did you ever know the middle sister, Miss Maude Barrington?'

Something hardened in Mrs Dowson's face and her eyes were chill. 'I did. But if you have come to say something uncomplimentary about her, I would thank you not to. I know she was a little unruly, and perhaps she threw herself too fully into things, but she had a good heart, and it was all very long ago. I think one should take one's victories very lightly, and one's losses with silence and dignity, do you not agree, Mrs Ellison?'

How curious! Not at all what Mariah had expected. Mrs Dowson's eyes might be bright and cold, but they kindled a sudden new warmth in Mariah's mind.

'Indeed I do,' she said heartily. 'That is one of the reasons I felt an affection for Maude the moment I met her. It is one of the great sadnesses of my life that I knew her such a very short time.'

'I beg your pardon?' Mrs Dowson said huskily, her face now filled with alarm.

Even a week ago Mariah would have made a condescending reply to that. Now all she wanted to do was find some kinder way of telling the news.

'I am so sorry. Maude arrived home from abroad and because of other family commitments at her sister's house, she came and stayed with her cousin, Mr Joshua Fielding, who is also a relative of mine, hence my presence there. Maude died, quite peacefully in her sleep, three days ago.' She saw the undisguised pain in the old lady's face. 'I felt so very grieved I chose to take the news to her family in person, rather than merely send some written message,' she concluded, 'which is how I come to be still staying with them now. I am doing what little I can to help.'

'Oh dear,' Mrs Dowson said, shaking her head a little. 'I assumed it was no more than another of Agnes's chills, or whatever it is she has. How stupid of me. One should not assume. This is a deep loss.' Suddenly the tears filled her eyes. 'I'm so sorry,' she apologised.

Mariah did not find it absurd that after forty years Mrs Dowson should still grieve so keenly. Time does not cloud certain memories. Bright days from youth, laughter and friendship can remain.

But crass as it seemed, it was also an opportunity that she could not afford to ignore. 'Did you know her well, before she left to travel abroad?' she asked.

'Oh, yes,' Mrs Dowson smiled. 'I knew all the girls then. My husband was a curate, just young in his ministry. Very earnest, you know, as dedicated men can be. I rather think Maude overwhelmed him. She was so fierce in her love for Arthur Harcourt. And, of course, Arthur was quite the dashing young man about town. He was extraordinarily handsome, and he knew it. But he could hardly fail to. If he'd crooked a finger at any of the girls in the south of England they'd have followed him. I might have myself, if I'd thought he meant it. But I was never very pretty, and I was happy enough with Walter. He was genuine. I rather thought Arthur wasn't.'

'Not sincere? Was he simply playing with Maude?' Suddenly Mariah's liking for Arthur Harcourt evaporated as if she had torn the smiling mask off and seen rotten flesh underneath.

'Oh, no,' Mrs Dowson said quickly. 'That was where Walter and I disagreed. He thought Arthur loved Bedelia. He called them a perfect match. Something of an idealist, my husband. Thought beauty was bone deep, not just a chance of colouring and half an inch here and there, and, of course, confidence. Self-belief, you know? Imagine how the map of the world might have been changed if Cleopatra's nose had been half an inch longer! Then Caesar might not have fallen in love with her, or Mark Antony either.'

Mariah was carried along in a hurricane of thought.

'I'm so sorry,' Mrs Dowson apologised again. 'Walter always said my mind was totally undisciplined. I told him that was not so at all, simply that it moved in a different pattern from his. Bedelia Barrington could twist him around her little finger! And half the men in the county, too. Poor Zachary never got over it, which is such a shame. Agnes was the better girl, if only she could have believed that herself!'

Mariah did not interrupt her. The tea arrived. Mrs Dowson poured, and passed the mince pies and jam tarts.

'Bedelia thought she was glamorous, Agnes was dull and Maude was plain and eccentric. Because of her confidence, far too many people believed that she must be right.'

'But she was not . . . ?'

'Certainly she was,' Mrs Dowson contradicted her. 'But only because we allowed her to be. Except Maude. She knew Bedelia's beauty was of no real value. No warmth in it, do you see?'

'But she fell in love with Arthur? So much so that she could not bear it when he came to his senses and married Bedelia after all?' Mariah deliberately chose her words provocatively.

'I used to think he lost his senses again,' Mrs Dowson

argued. 'I was furious with Maude for not fighting for the man she loved. Fancy simply giving up and running away like that! Off to North Africa, and then Egypt and Persia. Riding horses in the desert, and camels too, for all I can say. Lived in tents and gave what was left of her heart to the Persians.'

'She wrote to you!' Mariah was astonished, and delighted. Maude had had a friend here who had cared for her over the years and kept her in touch with home.

'Of course,' Mrs Dowson said indignantly. 'She never told me why she left, but I came to realise it was a matter of honour, and must not ever be discussed. She did what she believed to be the right thing. But I don't think that she ever stopped loving Arthur.'

New ideas began to form in Mariah's mind. 'Mrs Dowson, do you know why Maude chose to come home now, after so long?' she asked. 'Did she have any . . . any anxieties about her health?'

'Not that she confided in me.' Mrs Dowson frowned. 'She was certainly afraid, a little oppressed by the thought of returning after so long. But the gentleman she had cared for in Persia, and who had loved her, had died. She told me that. It grieved her very much, and it also meant that she had no reason for remaining there any more. In fact, she implied that without his protection it would be unwise for her to do so. I do not know their relationship. I never asked and she never told me, but it was not regular, as you and I would use the term.'

'I see. Was Bedelia aware of this?' Was that the scandal she was afraid might come to Lord Woollard's ears – even perhaps quite frankly told by Maude, in order to shock? After Bedelia's coolness over the years, and the fact that it was she Arthur had married, whatever his reason, it would not be unnatural now if Maude had been unable to resist at least preventing her sister from becoming Lady Harcourt. Mariah asked Mrs Dowson as much.

'She may have been tempted,' Mrs Dowson replied. 'But she would not have done it. Maude never bore a grudge. That was Bedelia.'

'Was Bedelia not very much in love with Arthur, even before Maude returned from caring for her aunt?' Mariah asked.

'Maude did tell you a great deal, didn't she?' Mrs Dowson observed.

Mariah merely smiled.

'However much Maude had despised Bedelia, she would never have hurt Arthur,' Mrs Dowson continued. 'As I said, she never stopped loving him. And I refer to that emotion that seeks the best for the other, the honour and happiness and inward spiritual journey; not the hunger to possess at all costs, the joy for oneself in their company and the feeling that they are happy only when they are with you. That is Bedelia, all about winning. And poor Agnes was concerned she was always going to be no more than second best.'

'Then why was Arthur so foolish?' Mariah marvelled.

'Was he really blinded by mere physical . . . oh.' A far simpler
and more understandable answer came to her mind. She saw
that Mrs Dowson was watching her intently. She felt the heat
in her cheeks as if she could read her thoughts.

'I do not know,' Mrs Dowson said quietly. 'But I believe
Maude did, and that is why Bedelia was very happy that she
should remain in Persia for the rest of her life.'

The idea became firmer in Mariah's mind. It made sense
of what was otherwise outside the character and nature of
the people she had observed. Looking at Mrs Dowson, she
was certain she had guessed the same answer. She smiled
across at her. 'How very sad,' she said gently, aware of what
an absurd understatement that was. 'Poor Arthur.' She hesitated. 'And poor Zachary.'

'And Agnes,' Mrs Dowson added. 'But above all, I wish
that Maude had not . . . not suffered so.'

'But she made the best of it,' Mariah said with an intensity of feeling, an absolute conviction that welled up inside
her, driving away all doubt.

Mrs Dowson nodded. 'Maude always knew how to live.
She knew the worst was there and she accepted the pain as
part of the truth of things, but she chose to see the best also,
and to find the joy in variety. She did not close herself off
from the richness of experience. I think that was her gift. I
shall miss her terribly.'

'Even though I knew her only a short while, I shall miss
her also,' Mariah confessed. 'But I am profoundly grateful

that I did know her. And . . . and gratitude is something I have not felt lately. Simply to have that back is a . . .' She did not know how to finish. She sniffed, pulled her emotions together with an effort, then rose to her feet. 'But I have something to do. I must return to Snave and attend to it. Thank you very much for your hospitality, Mrs Dowson, and even more for the understanding you have given me. May I wish you the joy of the season, and remembrance of all that is good in the past, together with hope for the future.'

Mrs Dowson rose also. 'Why, how graciously put, Mrs Ellison. I shall endeavour to remember that. May I wish you joy also, and safety in your journey, both in the body and in the spirit? Happy Christmas.'

Outside it was beginning to snow, white flurries on the wind. So far it was only dusting the ground, but the heavy pall of cloud to the north made it apparent that there was a great deal more to come. Whether she wanted to or not, Mariah would be unlikely to be able to return to St Mary in the Marsh today. That was a good thing. What she had to do would be best done in the evening, when they were all together after dinner. It would be uncomfortable, extremely so. She felt a sinking in her stomach as she sat in the pony trap, wrapped against the snow. The biting wind was behind her and the roar of the sea breaking on the shore growing fainter as they moved inland between the wide, flat fields, beginning to whiten.

She was afraid. She admitted it to herself. She was afraid

of unpleasantness, even physical attack, although she expected any attack to be secret, disguised, as the one on Maude had been. Even more than that, and it surprised her, she was afraid of not doing it well.

But then, like Agnes, she had regarded herself as a failure most of her life. She had lived a lie, always pretending to be a highly respectable woman, even aggressively so, married to a man who had died relatively young and left her grieving since her late forties, unable to recover from the loss.

In truth she had married wretchedly, and his death had released her, at least on the outside. She had never allowed herself to be released in her own mind, and worse still, in her heart. She had kept up the lie, to save her pride.

Of course no one ever needed to know the details, but she could have been honest with herself, and it would slowly have spread through her manner, her beliefs, and in the end the way she had seen and been seen by others.

Maude Barrington had suffered a monstrous injustice. She had borne it apparently without bitterness. If it had marred an earlier part of her life, perhaps when she first went abroad, she had healed her own spirit from the damage and gone on to live a passionate and adventurous life. Perhaps it had never been comfortable, but what was comfort worth? Bitterness, blame and self-hatred were never comfortable either. And perhaps they were also not as safe as she had once imagined. They were a slow-growing disease within, killing inch by inch.

It was snowing quite hard now, lying thick and light on the ground, beginning to drift on the windward side of the furrows in the fields after their winter ploughing, and on the trunks of the trees. The wind was blowing too hard for the snow to stay on the branches as they swayed against the sky. There was little sound from the pony's hoofs because the ground was blanketed already, just the deep moan of the wind and the creak of the wheels. It was a hard, beautiful world, invigorating, ice-cold, and on every side, sweet- and sharp-smelling from the sea, infinitely wide.

Mariah arrived back at Snave before she was really ready, but there was no help for it. And maybe she would never feel as if it were time. She allowed the stable boy to assist her, and to his surprise thanked him for his care.

Inside she took off her cape and shawl and was very glad to be in the warmth again. Her hands were almost numb from the cold and her face was stinging, her eyes watering, but she had never felt more intensely alive. She was terrified, and yet there was an unmistakable bubble of courage inside her, as if something of Maude's vitality and hunger for life had been bequeathed to her.

She was too late for luncheon, and too excited to eat much anyway. Cook had prepared a tray for her with soup and new, warm bread, and that was really all she required. She thanked her sincerely, with a compliment, and after finishing it all, went upstairs with the excuse that she wished to lie down. In reality she wanted to prepare herself for the evening. It was going to be one of the biggest of her life, perhaps her only real achievement. It would require all the nerve and the intelligence she possessed. There was in her mind no doubt of the truth now. Proving it would be altogether another matter, but if she did not attempt it, whatever it cost her, then she would have failed the last chance that fate had offered.

Mariah dressed very carefully, in the housekeeper's best black gown, and thanked the maid. It seemed appropriate. She was going to be a different person from the woman she had been as long as she could clearly remember. She was going to be brave, face all the ugliness, the shame and the failure and be gentle towards them, because she understood them intimately. She had been a liar herself, and every stupid ugly corner of it was familiar. She had been a coward, and its corroding shroud had covered every part of her life. She had tried to touch other people's lives with her own meanness of spirit, her belief in failure. There was no victory in that. One could spoil others, dirty them, damage what could have been whole. Now she could touch all their wounds with pity, but none of them could deceive her.

She regarded herself in the glass. She looked different from the way she was accustomed. It was more than the dress that was not her own; the face also was not the one that had been hers for so long. There was colour in her skin. Her eyes were brighter. Most of all the sulk had gone from her lips, and the lines seemed to be curving upward, not down.

Ridiculous! She had never been pretty, and she wasn't now. If she did not know better she would think she had been imbibing rather too freely of the Christmas spirit, of that nature that comes in a bottle!

She straightened her skirt a last time, and went down to join the family for dinner. Tomorrow she would leave. She would probably have to, even if the snow were up to the eaves! There was something exhilarating, and a little mad in casting the last die, crossing the Rubicon, if she were remembering her schoolroom history correctly. It was war! Triumph or disaster, because she could not stop until it was over.

She was a few minutes late, as she had intended, and dinner was announced almost as soon as she joined her hosts. They all went into the dining room. It was now looking even more festive, with scarlet berries intertwined in the wreaths and the swags along the mantelpiece, all tied with gold ribbons. There were scarlet candles on the table, though they were not yet lit, and everything seemed to be touched with light from the chandeliers.

'I hope you are recovered from your journey, Mrs Ellison?' Arthur asked with concern. 'I'm afraid the weather turned most unpleasant before you were able to return.'

'I should not have allowed you to go,' Bedelia added. 'I had not realised it would take you so long.'

'It was entirely my own fault,' Mariah replied. 'I could have been back earlier, and I should have, for the stable boy and the pony's sake, if nothing else. To tell you the truth, the ride back was very beautiful. I have not been out in a snow-storm for so long that I had forgotten how amazing it is. The sense of the power and magnitude of nature is very marvellous.'

'What a refreshing view,' Arthur said, then suddenly the sadness filled his eyes, overwhelming him. 'You remind me of Maude.' He stopped, unable to continue.

It was the greatest compliment Mariah had ever received, but she could not afford to stop and savour it now.

She continued with what she had intended to say, regardless of their responses. She even ignored the butler and the footman serving the soup.

'Thank you, Mr Harcourt. The more I learn of Maude, the more do I appreciate how very much that means. I know that for you it is as profound as it could be, and I wish more than you can be aware of to live up to it.'

Bedelia was startled, then her mouth curled in a smile more of disdain than amusement. 'We all grieve for Maude, Mrs Ellison, but there is no requirement for you to cater to our family perception with such praise.' She left the implied adjective 'fulsome' unsaid, but it hung in the air.

'Oh, I'm not!' Mariah said candidly, her eyes wide. 'Maude was a most remarkable person. I learned far more of just how amazing from Mrs Dowson. That, I'm afraid, is why I stayed so long.'

Bedelia was stiff, her shoulders like carved ivory beneath her black taffeta gown. 'Mrs Dowson is sentimental,' she replied coolly. 'A vicar's widow and obliged to see the best in people.'

'Perhaps the vicar did,' Mariah corrected her. 'Mrs Dowson certainly does not. She is quite capable of seeing pride, greed, selfishness, and other things, like cowardice in particular.' She smiled at Agnes. 'The acceptance of failure because one does not have the courage to face what one is afraid of, and pay the price in comfort, that is sometimes necessary for success.'

The blood drained from Agnes's face, leaving her ashen. Her spoon slithered into her soup dish and she ignored it.

Zachary started to speak, and then choked on whatever it was he had been going to say.

It was Randolph who came to her rescue. 'That sounds extremely harsh, Mrs Ellison. How on earth would Mrs Dowson be in a position to know anything of that sort about anybody? And what she did know must have come to her in a privileged position, and therefore should not be repeated.'

'Most unchristian,' Clara added.

'It can be very difficult to recognise the right thing to do, at times,' Mariah continued, grateful for the extraordinary ease with which the opportunities she needed were opening up for her. 'But I must not misrepresent Mrs Dowson. Actually she said nothing, except to praise Maude's love of beauty, her laughter, and above all her courage to make the best of her life, even after so great a sacrifice, which was given silently and with the utmost dignity.'

Zachary looked totally confused. Arthur was pale; his breathing seemed painful. Bedelia was as white as Agnes now, and her hands on her lap were clenched. No one ate.

'I am not sure what you imagine you are referring to, Mrs Ellison,' Bedelia said icily. 'It appears you are a lonely woman with nothing to do, and you have concerned yourself in our family's affairs in a way which exceeds even your imagined duty to Maude, whom you barely met. Your meddlesomeness has run away with you. I think we had better find a way to return you to St Mary in the Marsh tomorrow, regardless of the weather. I am sure that would be better for all of us.'

Randolph blushed scarlet.

It was Arthur who spoke. 'Bedelia, that is unnecessary. I apologise, Mrs Ellison. I don't know what Maude told you, but I think you must have misunderstood her.'

'She told me nothing,' Mariah said, meeting his eyes. 'She would never betray you like that! And surely by now you must know beyond any question at all that she would not betray Bedelia either! She did not come here to cause any kind of trouble. The man who had loved her and protected her in Persia died, and she could no longer remain there. She came back home because she wished to. Perhaps she even imagined that after all these years she would be welcome. Which, of course, was an error. Quite obviously she was not.'

'You have no right to say that!' Clara cut in. 'She had been living in the desert, in tents and by campfires, like a . . . a

117

gypsy! And with a foreign man to whom she was not married! We could hardly have her in the house at the same time as Lord Woollard! My father-in-law has given more to society than you have any idea. This peerage would have been not only a just reward but an opportunity to do even more good. We could not jeopardise that!'

'And it would, in time, have made you Lady Harcourt,' Mariah added. 'With all that that means. Of course you did not wish to lose such a prize.'

'Oh, no . . . I . . .' Clara faded into silence. She had the grace to be ashamed.

'Stuff and nonsense!' Bedelia snapped. 'You overstep yourself, Mrs Ellison. Your behaviour is disgraceful!'

'She came home because she had nowhere else to go?' Agnes asked, her face pinched with sorrow. 'We should have forgiven her, Bedelia. It was a very long time ago.'

'Bedelia does not forgive,' Mariah answered Agnes. 'Not that there was anything of Maude's that needed pardon. Tragically there are some people who can never forgive a gift, especially from someone who is aware of their vulnerability. Sometimes it is harder to forgive a gift than an injury, because you have incurred a debt, in your own eyes you have lost control, and your superiority.'

There was an electric silence.

'Those who themselves do not forgive find it impossible to believe that others do,' Mariah went on. 'So they expect vengeance where there is none, and strike out to defend themselves from a blow that exists only in their own guilty imaginations.'

Arthur leaned forward. 'I think you had better stop speaking in riddles, Mrs Ellison. I have very little idea of what you are talking about . . .'

'Neither has she!' Bedelia said tartly. 'Really, Arthur, you should have more sense than to encourage her. Can't you see that she has been drinking? Let us speak of something civilised and stop descending into personal remarks. It is extremely vulgar.' She spoke as if that were the end of the matter.

Arthur drew in his breath, but it was Agnes who answered. She looked at Mariah directly. 'Was Maude ill? Did she know she was going to die, and that was why she came home at last? To make peace?'

'No,' Mariah replied with authority. 'As I said, there was nothing to keep her in Persia any more, nor was it safe.'

'She had made enemies, no doubt,' Bedelia observed. 'You did not say that this man was married to someone else, but, knowing Maude, I have no doubt that it was true.'

'Oh, Bedelia, you should forgive her that!' Agnes pleaded. 'It was forty years ago! And she is gone now. It's Christmas!'

'Don't be so feeble!' Bedelia accused her. 'Wrong does not suddenly become right just because of the season.'

Agnes blushed scarlet.

'Of course it doesn't,' Mariah agreed vehemently. 'Some debts can be forgiven, but there are some which have to be paid, one way or another.'

119

'I don't care for your opinion, Mrs Ellison,' Bedelia said frigidly.

'There is no reason why you should,' again Mariah agreed with her. 'But you care about your family's opinions. In the end it is really all you have. That, and the knowledge within yourself, of course. Perhaps that is why Maude was happy, in the deepest sense. She knew she was loved, and no matter what the cost, she had done the right thing.'

'I have no idea what you are talking about!'

'Yes you have. You are probably the only one who does have.' Nothing was going to stop Mariah. 'When you were a young woman, and even more beautiful than you are now, Mrs Harcourt,' she glanced at Zachary, 'he fell in love with you. And like many young people, you did not deny yourselves the pleasure of love.'

Bedelia hissed in her breath, but the shame in Zachary's face made her denial impossible.

'But then Mr Harcourt came along, and he was a far better catch, so you went after him instead,' Mariah continued relentlessly. 'And you caught him – at least his admiration for your beauty, and a certain physical appetite. You also did not deny yourselves. After all, you fully intended to marry him. Which would all have gone very well, had not Maude returned home, and Mr Harcourt fell truly in love with her.'

Bedelia's eyes on her were like daggers.

Mariah ignored them, but her heart was pounding almost in her throat. If she were wrong, catastrophically, insanely wrong, she would be ruined for ever. Her mouth was dry, her voice rasping. 'You were furious that Maude, of all people, should take your lover, but there was worse to follow. You learned that you were with child. Mr Sullivan's, of course. But it could have been Mr Harcourt's, for all he knew. That gave you your perfect weapon for regaining everything. You told him. Being a man of honour, in spite of his lapse of self-control, he broke off his relationship with Maude, whom he truly loved, as she loved him, and he married you. He paid a bitter price for his self-indulgence. So did your sister, rather than allow you to be shamed.'

There were gasps of breath, the clink of cutlery, even the crock of a breaking glass stem.

'That is what you cannot forgive – that you wronged her,' she went on regardless. 'And she sacrificed her happiness for yours – and perhaps for Mr Harcourt's honour. Although I believe it was actually Mr Sullivan's, in fact.'

Arthur stared at Bedelia, a stunned and terrible look in his eyes. 'Randolph is not mine, and you know it?' he said very quietly.

'Are ... are you sure?' Agnes asked. Then she looked more closely at Bedelia, and did not ask again.

'What does she mean, that you could not forgive?' Arthur asked Bedelia.

'I have no idea!' Bedelia replied. 'She is an inquisitive, meddling old woman who listens at doors and hears half-stories, gossips with other old women who should know better, and apparently listened to Maude's self-delusions of her own romantic youth.'

'It wasn't a delusion,' Arthur told her very quietly. 'I loved Maude as I have never loved anyone else in my life, before or since. But I could not marry her because you told me that you were carrying my child. I can't blame you for that – it was my doing as much as yours. Nor can I blame Zachary. He was no worse than I, and, by heaven, you were beautiful. But Maude was funny and kind. She was brave and warm and honest, and she was generous with life, with her own spirit. Her beauty would have lasted for ever, and grown with time rather than fading. I knew it then, and I was proved right when she came back, even after forty years, which were like a lifetime while she was gone, and nothing at all once she returned.'

'Oh, Arthur!' Agnes breathed out. 'How terrible for you.'

Zachary was looking at her with amazement, as if he did not completely recognise her.

'I found the rest of the peppermint water,' Mariah said in the silence.

'I beg your pardon?' Arthur frowned.

Mariah wavered for an instant. Should she tell them, or was this enough? But would it last? There would be no further chance. She turned to Bedelia and saw the fury in her eyes.

'You told Maude when you gave her the macadamia nuts, which are so indigestible to some of us, that you had very little peppermint water, just the end of one bottle, sufficient for a single dose. But actually you had plenty. There is some in my room, and some in the other guest rooms also. A nice courtesy, especially over a festive season when we will all eat a little heavily.'

'What has that to do with anything at all?' Clara demanded. 'Why are we talking about peppermint water? Are you quite mad?'

'I wish I were,' Mariah answered. 'It would be so much less ugly an answer than the truth. I don't eat macadamia nuts myself. They give me indigestion . . .'

Zachary was staring at her as if he could not believe his ears.

Agnes looked appalled.

'But peppermint water would help,' Mariah carried on. 'Unless, of course, it were laced with foxglove leaves. Then it would kill. Most of us know that who have ever arranged flowers. There are a few one must be careful of, especially with children about: laburnum, monkshood, belladonna and, of course, foxgloves. Such handsome flowers, but the distilled juice can cause the heart to fail. It is used in medicine to slow it down if it is racing, but only a very little, naturally.'

'That is a wicked thing to suggest!' Clara was horrified. 'How . . . how dare you?'

Randolph touched her gently. 'There is no need to be afraid, my dear. She could not possibly prove it.' He gulped. 'Could you?'

Mariah looked at him and realised it was a question. 'I

don't know,' she replied. 'I had not considered trying to, although it might not be too difficult. I don't think that is what matters. It is knowing the truth that is important. It gives you the freedom to do whatever you choose to, knowing right from wrong.' She turned to Arthur, waiting for him to speak.

But he was not looking at her. His gaze did not move from Bedelia's face, and he read in it the fear and the hatred that betrayed her. Whatever she had said, he would know what she had done.

Randolph was staring at his mother with horror and pity in his face, and a revulsion he could not hide. He turned swiftly to Zachary, then, embarrassed, away again. Zachary was looking at him with wonder, and an intensity quite naked in his eyes.

Arthur sighed. He spoke to Mariah as if Bedelia had ceased to exist. 'You mentioned a garden in Persia that Maude described to you as if she loved it. Have you any idea where it was, exactly?'

'No, but I believe Mrs Dowson would know,' Mariah replied. 'Maude wrote to her quite regularly. I imagine she would be happy to tell you.'

'Good. I have a great desire to see it, since she loved it so much. You made it sound marvellous also, Mrs Ellison, and for that I shall always be grateful to you. The truth you have shown us is terrible, but deep as it cuts, a clean wound will heal, in time.'

'You . . . you can't go to Persia now, Papa . . . I mean . . .'
Randolph faltered and stopped.

Arthur smiled at him, gently and with great affection. 'You
will always be my son in spirit, Randolph, and I will always
love you as such. But I can go to Persia and I will. I shall
write to Lord Woollard and decline a peerage. I may return
from Persia one day, and I may not. The estate will provide
for your mother. Please see that Mrs Ellison is safely returned
to St Mary in the Marsh tomorrow. Now I shall wish you
good night.' He rose to his feet. He was still a startlingly
handsome man, but it was his dignity that remained in the
mind. 'And goodbye,' he added, before turning and leaving
the room without looking behind him. He did not once glance
at Bedelia.

Zachary reached out his hand to Agnes, and very slowly,
as if uncertain that it could be true, she took it.

Reluctantly Mariah abandoned her dinner and excused
herself also. It was quite impossible to remain. She had shown
them the truth. What they did with it she should not influ-
ence, only hope.

Upstairs in her bedroom she sank down into the chair.
Suddenly her legs were weak and she found she was trembling. Had she done enough? Should she have tried harder
to prove something that would stand the test of trial and the
law?

As it was now, the family knew the truth. There could be
no denying that. Arthur would leave, perhaps for ever. Bedelia

would probably never see him again. People would know, in the way that they do. They would look at her and whisper. There would be speculation, most of it ugly. The kindest she would receive would be pity, and that would be the most painful of all to a woman like Bedelia. She would see it in their glances in the street, the half-hidden smiles.

Gradually perhaps even some of the truth would emerge, but imagination would be more colourful, and crueller. Agnes and Zachary would be happy with each other at last, and perhaps with Randolph too, and Clara. Old Mrs Dowson would understand a great deal. She might be discreet, but Bedelia would know that she knew, and would never allow Maude's name to be blackened.

Bedelia would be provided for, waited on, but starved of friendship or admiration. No one would care how beautiful she had been, or how clever. She would be alone, a woman unloved.

At a glance, that was a gentler punishment than trial, and possibly the gallows, or possibly a verdict of innocence. But it would be more certain, and far, far longer. She would taste it for the rest of her life.

But the others would be happy, perhaps for the first time in their lives.

Mariah stopped shaking and sat still, slowly beginning to smile, even if there was sadness in it, and pity.

In the morning Zachary drove her back through the deepening snow to St Mary in the Marsh. He did not speak much, but she felt a great certainty that he had at last realised that Agnes was not a paler, second-best version of Bedelia, but a kinder if less brave person, a gentler, more generous one, who might now, at last, find the courage to be the best in herself. And she had always truly loved him.

'Thank you, Mrs Ellison,' he said as the trap rounded the last corner through the dazzling snow and she saw Joshua and Caroline's house blazing with lights.

'I hope you will be happy,' she replied, meaning it far more than the simple words could convey.

'I . . . I understand why you and Maude were such good friends,' he said earnestly. 'Even in so short a time. You are like her. You have such courage to tell the truth, however difficult, and such joy for life. I am amazed at your compassion for even the weakest of us. I imagine you will have a wonderful Christmas, because you will make it so. But I wish it for you just the same.'

'I will,' she assured him as they drew up in front of the door. It opened and Joshua came down the step and across the grass to the trap to assist her. 'I shall have the best Christmas of my life,' she went on, still speaking to Zachary. 'I am beginning to understand what it truly means.'

'Welcome home, Mama-in-law,' Joshua said with surprise, lifting his eyebrows. He gave her his arm and she alighted.

'Thank you, Joshua.' She smiled at him. 'Happy Christmas, my dear. I have wonderful things to tell you, brave and beautiful things, when I can think how to find words for them. About hope, and honour, and what love really means. Your Aunt Maude was a very wonderful woman. She has given me the greatest gift of all – an understanding of Christmas itself.'

'Yes, I see that,' Joshua said with sudden conviction. 'It is perfectly plain. Happy Christmas, Mama-in-law.'

Headline hope you have enjoyed reading Anne Perry's
A CHRISTMAS GUEST, and invites you to sample the
beginning of A CHRISTMAS SECRET, another novel
by Anne Perry, available now from Headline.

Clarice Corde leaned back in her seat as the train pulled out of the station in a cloud of steam. Smuts flew, and engine roared as it gathered speed. The rain beat against the window and she could barely see the glistening rooftops of London. It was 14 December 1890, ten days before Christmas Eve. She had been married little more than a year, and she was far from used to being a vicar's wife. Neither obedience nor tact came to her except with a considerable effort, but she made it for Dominic's sake.

She glanced sideways at him now and saw him deep in thought. She knew he was concerned for his ability to rise to this opportunity they had been offered so unexpectedly. The elderly Reverend Mr Wynter had taken a richly deserved holiday; therefore his church, in the small village of Cottisham, needed someone to stand in for him to care for his flock over Christmas.

Dominic had seized the chance. He had been a widower who had abandoned a self-indulgent life and embraced the ministry somewhat late. Perhaps no one but Clarice saw beyond his handsome face and ease of manner to the doubts beneath. She loved him the more fiercely because she knew he understood his own weaknesses as well as the power of his dreams.

He looked up and smiled at her. Once again she was warmed by amazement that he should have chosen her: the awkward sister, the one with the tactless tongue and the disastrous sense of humour rather than any of the reliable and more conventional beauties eager for his attention.

This chance to go to Cottisham, in the county of Hertfordshire, was the greatest Christmas gift they could have been given. It was an escape from serving under the Reverend Mr Spindlewood in the bleak area of industrial London to which Dominic had been sent as curate.

How could she reassure him that his new parishioners expected only patience, and that he should be there to listen and comfort, to assure them of the message of Christmas, and peace on earth?

She reached her hand across and touched his arm, tightening her fingers for a moment. 'It will be good,' she said firmly. 'And being in the country will be fun.'

He smiled at her, his dark eyes bright, knowing what she meant to tell him.

The village was indeed beautiful, even though it boasted little more than a wide green with a duck pond and houses all around it. Many of the dwellings were thatched, their bare winter gardens neatly tidied. Perhaps half a dozen narrow roads twisted away into the surrounding woods and the fields beyond. The church was Saxon: slate-roofed, with a square tower rising high against the wind-torn clouds.

The carriage that had brought them from the station drew up in front of the rambling stone vicarage. The driver unloaded their cases on to the gravel, and drove away.

Clarice looked at the closed door, then at the fine Georgian windows. It was a beautiful house, but it seemed oddly blind, as if it were oblivious to their arrival, and they would knock on the oak door in vain. This was to be their home, and Dominic's challenge and opportunity would be to preach and to minister without supervision, or the constant meddling of the Reverend Mr Spindlewood. Clarice knew she must behave with enthusiasm now, whatever doubt or loneliness she felt. That was what faith was about. Anyone can be cheerful when they are fresh and the sun is shining.

She looked at Dominic once, then marched up to the front door and banged briskly with the lion's-head knocker.

There was total silence from inside.

'Stay here with the boxes,' Dominic said quietly. 'I'll go to the nearest house. They must have left the keys with someone.'

But before he could go more than a dozen steps a stout woman, with hair piled up on her head in an untidy knot, came bustling along the road. She struggled to hold a shawl around her shoulders against the wind.

'All right! All right! I'm coming,' she called out. 'No hurry! It ain't snowin' yet. You must be the Reverend Mr Corde. An' Mrs Corde, I take it?' She stopped in front of them and looked Clarice up and down dubiously. 'I s'pose you know how to care for a house, an' all?' she said in a tone close to accusation. 'I'm Mrs Wellbeloved. I look after the vicar, but I can't do no more for you than a bit o' the heavy work, 'cos I've got family coming for Christmas, an' I need me holiday too. In't good for a body to work all the days o' the year, an' it in't right to expect it.'

'Of course we don't expect it,' Clarice agreed, although she had in fact expected exactly that. 'If you show me where to find everything, and assist with the laundry, I'm sure that will be most satisfactory.'

Mrs Wellbeloved looked more or less mollified. She produced a large key from her pocket, unlocked the door and led the way in.

Clarice followed her, pleasantly surprised by the warmth of the house, even though the vicar had been gone for a couple of days. It smelled of lavender, beeswax and the faint, earthy perfume of chrysanthemums. Everything looked clean: the wooden floor, the hall table, the doors leading off to left and right, the stairs going up towards a wide landing. There was a large vase of branches and leaves of gold and bronze on the floor. For all her lack of grace, Mrs Wellbeloved seemed to be an excellent housekeeper.

'You'll be liking it here,' she said more to Dominic than

to Clarice. It sounded something of an order. 'Folks know how to behave decent. Come to church regular and give to the poor. Won't be nothing for you to do but your duty. Just keep it right for the vicar to come back to. I'm sure he's left you a list of them as needs visiting, but if he hasn't, I can tell you.' She opened the sitting-room door to show them a graceful room with a wide fireplace and bay window, and then closed the door again. 'You'll be takin' all services regular,' she went on, walking quickly towards the kitchen. 'An' you won't be wantin' the sexton, but if you do, he's first on the right on the Glebe Road. Gravedigger's two down beyond.'

'Thank you, Mrs Wellbeloved.' Dominic avoided meeting Clarice's eyes, and answered with as straight a face as he could manage.

'I'll be in reg'lar for the heavy stuff, 'ceptin' Christmas Day, an' Boxin' Day, o' course,' Mrs Wellbeloved continued. 'You'll have enough coal an' coke an' likely enough kindlin', but if you haven't you can go walk in the woods an' pick up plenty. Works best of all if you dry it proper first. An' you'll walk Harry too. I can't be doin' that.'

'Harry?' Dominic asked, puzzled.

'Harry.' She looked at him witheringly. 'The dog! Didn't the vicar tell you about Harry? Retriever, he is. Good as gold, if you treat him right. An' Etta. But you don't need to do nothin' for her, 'cept scraps and stuff, an' milk. She'll fend for herself.'

Clarice made a quick guess. 'Etta's a cat?'

Mrs Wellbeloved looked appeased for their ignorance. 'Right good little mouser, she is. Plain as you like, but clever. Capture 'em all in the end.' She said it with satisfaction, as if she identified with the animal, and were in some oblique way describing herself as well.

Clarice could not help smiling. 'Thank you. I am sure we shall get along excellently. Thank you for showing us in. We shall have a cup of tea, and then unpack.'

'There's everything you'll need for today,' Mrs Wellbeloved nodded. 'Game pie in the pantry, an' plenty o' vegetables, such as there is this time o' year. You'll need onions. Vicar loved 'em. Hot onion soup best thing in the world for a cold, he said. Smells worse 'n whisky, but at least you're sober.' She gave Dominic a hard, level look.

He returned it unflinchingly, and then slowly smiled.

Mrs Wellbeloved grunted, then a pink blush spread up her face and she turned away. 'Handsome is as handsome does,' she muttered under her breath.

Clarice thanked her again and saw her to the door. She was ready to be alone in her new, temporary home, and take stock of things. But first she wanted a cup of tea. It had been a long journey and it was close to the shortest day in the year. Storm clouds were looming up over the trees and the light was fading.

The house was everything she could have hoped. It had charm and individuality. The furniture was all well used, but also well cared for. Nothing really matched, as if each had been gathered as opportunity arose, and yet nothing appeared to be out of place. Oak, mahogany and walnut jostled together, and age had mellowed them all. Elizabethan carving did not clash with Georgian simplicity. Everything seemed to be useful, except for one small table with barley-twist legs, which was there, Clarice guessed, simply because it was liked.

The pictures on the walls were also obviously personal choice: a watercolour of Bamburgh Castle on the Northumberland coast, rising out of the pale sands with the North Sea beyond; a Dutch scene of fishing boats; half a dozen pencil sketches of bare trees; more winter fields and trees in pen and ink. She found them remarkably restful; her eye returned to them again and again. Upstairs she found another sketch, this time of the ruins of Rievaulx Abbey, bare columns and broken walls towering against the clouds.

'Look at this,' she called to Dominic, who was carrying the last case up to the boxroom. 'Isn't it lovely?'

He put the case away before coming to stand a little behind her, his arm around her shoulder. 'Yes,' he agreed, examining the picture carefully. 'I like it very much.' He peered at the signature. 'It's his own! Did you see that?'

'His own?' she asked.

'The bishop told me he painted,' he replied. 'He didn't say how good he was, though. That has both power and grace to it. At least I think so. I'm looking forward to meeting him, when he comes back.'

Clarice caught the edge of ruefulness in his voice. Those three weeks would go by too quickly, and then they would have to return to London, and Mr Spindlewood. Before that time Dominic must somehow show that he was wise enough, gentle enough, and patient in listening to care for the village alone. He must be passionate and original in his sermons, not only to hold interest but to feed the heart with the special message of Christmas. She knew this mattered to him intensely, and that his belief in himself wavered. Only the total upheaval of his life had made him consider religious faith at all.

She also knew that empty words of assurance from her would not help. He already knew she believed in him, and took it for granted that it was born of her love more than any realism.

'I wonder if he'll do any more drawing while he's away this time,' she said. 'I don't even know where he's gone.'

Clarice awoke the next morning to stand shivering in her nightgown and drew the curtains open on to a glistening white world. The vicarage garden was surprisingly large and backed on to the woods. The trees were dusted with snow in wildly intricate patterns like heavy lace against a lead-grey sky, and the pale light gave it an eerie, luminous quality. She breathed out slowly in amazement at its beauty, momentarily forgetting to shiver.

She stared at it in rapture until suddenly she remembered

there was housework to be done: grates to clean out, fires to be laid and lit and breakfast to be cooked. And, of course, Harry and Etta to be fed. She could not afford to wait for Mrs Wellbeloved to come.

A little after ten o'clock, when Dominic was in the study reading some of the vicar's notes and trying to familiarise himself with the parish, there was a noise outside on the gravel drive. Harry came trotting out of the kitchen where he had been asleep by the stove. His nose was in the air and his plumed tail was waving; however, he did not bark.

Clarice snatched her apron off and went to open the door just as the knocker sounded. She pulled it wide to see a man standing just back from the step. He was a little above average height and apparently slender, although under the weight of his winter coat it was hard to tell. His face was fine-boned, not exactly handsome, but full of intelligence and a wry wit. His complexion was deep olive and his eyes had the liquid darkness that comes from the East. However, when he spoke his voice was as English as her own.

'How do you do, Mrs Corde? I am Peter Connaught.' He gestured vaguely behind him. 'From the manor house. I wanted to welcome you to the village.' He held out his hand, then glanced at the smooth, leather glove and apologised, pulling it off.

'How do you do, Mr Connaught?' she replied, smiling at him. 'That is most kind of you. May I offer you a cup of tea? It's terribly cold this morning.'

'That would be most welcome,' he accepted. 'I think it's going to be a hard Christmas – for weather, but I hope not for anything else.'

She stepped back and opened the door wider for him. He came in, glancing around as if perhaps the vicarage might have changed since he had been there last. Then he relaxed and smiled again, reassured. Did he think they would have moved things in a night?

She took his coat, and then showed him into the sitting room, grateful she had lit the fire early and it was pleasantly warm. She noticed how again he looked around, smiling at familiar things, the pictures, the way the furniture was arranged, the worn chairs with their colours blending.

'If you will excuse me, I shall tell my husband you are here. Then I shall bring tea.'

'Of course.' He inclined his head, rubbing his hands together. His polished boots were wet from the snow and the wind had whipped colour into his face.

She went to the study first and opened the door without knocking.

'Dominic, Mr Connaught from the manor house is in the sitting room. I'm just going to bring tea. It's very good of him to come, isn't it?'

He looked a little surprised. 'Yes. And very quick.' There was a note of apprehension in his voice.

Clarice heard it and was afraid he was anxious already that she might be too frank in her opinions, too quick not only to see a better way of doing something, but to say so. It had been known to happen before.

'I suppose I should call upon his wife. She will know all the women in the village and everything about them. He hasn't mentioned her,' she added, biting her lip and looking straight into his eyes. 'But I promise I shall behave perfectly. I will find her delightful and extremely competent, I promise you. Even if she is a blithering idiot with a tongue like a dose of vinegar! I really do promise.'

He stood up. 'Just don't expect me to watch you, and keep a straight face!' he warned, touching her cheek so lightly she barely felt it. 'Don't change too much! I wouldn't care to be Archbishop of Canterbury if I had to lose the person you are in order to do it!'

'Oh, if you were Archbishop of Canterbury,' she said cheerfully, 'I would probably say whatever I pleased! Everyone would be far too in awe of you to criticise me.'

He rolled his eyes, and went out to meet their guest.

Clarice went into the kitchen happily. To be loved for herself, with all her dreams and vulnerabilities, the mistakes and the virtues, was the highest prize in life, and she knew that.

When she returned with the tray of tea and biscuits she found both men seated by the fire talking. They rose immediately and Dominic took the tray from her and set it down. They exchanged the usual pleasantries. She poured and passed Connaught his cup, then Dominic.

'Sir Peter has been telling me a little about the village,' Dominic said, catching her eye. 'His family has been here for centuries.'

She felt herself blush. She had not known his title and had called him 'Mister' when she had asked him in. She wondered if he were offended. Normally she would not have cared, but all this mattered so much. She was not impressed with people's ancestors, but this was not the time to say so. She composed her face into an expression of interest. 'Really? How fortunate you are to have deep roots in such a lovely place.'

'Yes,' he agreed quickly. 'It gives me a great sense of belonging. And like all privileges, it carries certain obligations. But I believe they are a pleasure also. I was very sad when I learned that Mr Wynter was taking his holiday over Christmas, but now that we have you here, I am sure it will be as excellent as always. Christmas is a great time for healing rifts, forgiving mistakes, and welcoming wanderers home.'

'How very well you express it,' Dominic responded. 'Is that what Mr Wynter has said in the past, or your own feeling?'

Sir Peter looked slightly surprised, even momentarily disconcerted. 'My own. Why do you ask?'

'I thought it was so well phrased I might ask you if I could use it,' Dominic replied candidly. 'I would like to say something truly appropriate in my Watch Night sermon, which has to be as short as possible, yet still to have meaning. But

I cannot prepare it until I have at least a slight acquaintance with the village, and the people.'

Sir Peter leaned forward a little, a very slight frown between his dark brows. 'Did Mr Wynter not tell you at least a little about us, collectively and individually?'

Watching him, Clarice had the sudden certainty that the answer mattered to him far more than he wished them to know. There was a tension in the lines of his body, and the knuckles of his beautiful hands were white on his lap.

Dominic appeared not to have noticed. 'Unfortunately I never met him,' he answered. 'The request to fill this post came to me through the Bishop. I gather Mr Wynter's decision to take a holiday was made very quickly.'

'I see.' Sir Peter leaned back again and picked up his tea. 'That is a trifle awkward for you. Whatever I can do I shall be more than happy to. Call upon me at any time. Perhaps you will dine with me at the manor one evening, when you are settled in?' He looked at Clarice. 'I regret my hospitality will offer you no female company, since my mother has passed away, and I am not married, but I promise to show you much that is of interest, if you care for history, art or architecture. I can tell you stories of all manner of people good and evil, tragic and amusing, belonging to this village down the ages.'

She did not have to pretend interest. 'I think that would be infinitely more fun than any feminine gossip I can imagine,' she replied. 'And I will most certainly come.'

He looked pleased, as if the prospect excited him. Obviously he was enormously proud of his heritage and loved to share it, to entertain people, fill them with laughter and a little awe as well. He looked at Dominic. 'I see you have moved the chessboard. You do not play?'

Dominic glanced around. He clearly had no idea where the chessboard had been.

'You didn't?' Sir Peter said quickly. 'It was already gone when you came?'

'Yes. I haven't seen one.' He looked at Clarice questioningly.

'I haven't seen it either,' she said. 'Used Mr Wynter to play?'

A look of pain burned deep in Sir Peter's eyes, then with an effort he banished it. He swallowed the last of his tea. 'Yes. Yes, at one time. He had a particularly beautiful set. Not black and white so much as black and gold. The black was ebony, and the gold that extraordinary shade that yew wood sometimes achieves, almost metallic. Quite beautiful. Still . . .' He rose to his feet. 'It hardly matters. I just noticed because it was such a feature in the room. The light caught it, you know?'

'It sounds wonderful,' Clarice responded, because the silence demanded it, but her mind was filled with the certainty that his reason for asking was nothing like as casual as he had said. There was a depth of emotion in him that could not be explained by the mere absence of an artefact

144

of beauty. What more had it meant to him, and why did he conceal it?

She still wondered as she also rose to her feet and followed him to the door, thanking him again for his kindness in coming.

Mrs Wellbeloved arrived after luncheon, carrying a large bag of potatoes, which she set down on the kitchen table with a grunt of relief. 'You'll be needin' 'em,' she said.

'Thank you,' Clarice accepted, telling herself that Mrs Wellbeloved meant it kindly and it would be most ungracious to tell her that she would rather have gone to the village shop and bought them herself. Three weeks was such a short time to get to know people so she could help Dominic. 'Thank you,' she repeated. 'That was very thoughtful. We had a visitor this morning.' She carried the potatoes into the scullery, followed hopefully by the dog, who was ever optimistic about something new to eat.

'Come down here, did he?' Mrs Wellbeloved said, her eyes wide with interest. 'Well I never.' She picked up the long-handled broom and began to sweep the kitchen floor.

Clarice returned to the kitchen, Harry still on her heels.

'He said his family has been in the village for years,' she added, tidying one of the cupboards and setting jams, pickles, savoury jelly in some sort of order.

'Years!' Mrs Wellbeloved exclaimed. 'I should say centuries, more like. Since the Normans came, the way he tells it.'

'The Normans! Really?'

'Yes – 1066, you know?' Mrs Wellbeloved looked at her sceptically. How could she be the lady she pretended if she did not know that?

Clarice was amazed. 'That's terribly impressive!'

'Oh, he's impressed.' Mrs Wellbeloved bent awkwardly and picked up the modicum of dust from the floor, carefully pushing it into the dustpan. 'Come over with William the Conqueror, so he said, an' bin in this village since 1200. Everyone knows that.' She made an expression of disdain, then concealed it quickly, reaching for the bucket, putting it in the low, stone sink and turning on the tap.

'He didn't tell me that.' Clarice felt a need to defend him, although she had no idea why.

'Well, there's a surprise then.' Mrs Wellbeloved turned off the tap and heaved the bucket out. She looked at the floor sceptically. 'Don't seem too bad.'

'It isn't,' Clarice retorted. 'We haven't been here a whole day yet. I really don't think you need to do it.'

'P'raps you're right. I'll just do the table then. Got to keep the table clean.' She took the scrubbing brush off its rack, and a large box of yellow kitchen soap. 'Knew his father, Sir Thomas – he was a real gentleman, poor man.'

'Why? What happened to him?'

'Went abroad, he did.' Mrs Wellbeloved began scrubbing energetically, slopping water all over the place, wetting the entire surface of the table at once. 'Foreign parts somewhere

146

out east. Don't recall if he ever said where, exact. Fell in love and married. Then she died, when Sir Peter was only about five or six years old. Wonderful woman, she was, from all he says, an' very beautiful. Sir Thomas were so cut up by it he came home and never went back there, ever. Raised Peter himself, teaching him all about his family, the land, an' all that. Very close, but never got over her death. I s'pose Sir Peter didn't either. He never married.'

'There's time yet,' Clarice said quickly. 'He looks no more than in his forties. He'll want to keep the line going, the family, surely?'

Mrs Wellbeloved put her weight into the scrubbing, her lips tight, soapsuds flying. She stepped sideways and nearly fell over the dog. 'It's his duty,' she agreed. 'But he isn't doing it, for all that. Maybe that's what it was all about.'

'What what was all about?' Clarice asked unashamedly.

'Used to come here often,' Mrs Wellbeloved replied, wringing out a cloth with powerful, red-knuckled hands. 'Twice a week, most months. Played chess with the vicar reg'lar. Loved their game, they did. Then he stopped all of a sudden, about two years ago. Never came here since, except it were business, or with other folk. Vicar never said why, but then he wouldn't. Could keep other folk's secrets better than the grave, he could.'

'You mean they quarrelled?' Clarice felt a stab of disappointment. It seemed such a sad and stupid thing to do. 'What quarrel could be so bad, and last so long?'

Mrs Wellbeloved jerked upright, banging her elbow on the bucket, which was still on the table. She winced. 'Well, it wouldn't be Mr Wynter's fault, an' that's for certain. He was the best man that ever lived in the village, whether his family went back to the manor or the workhouse! Forgive anybody anything, he would, if it were against himself. Tried over and over to make it up with Sir Peter, but Sir Peter weren't having any of it.' She grunted fiercely. 'But the vicar would never say a thing were right if it weren't. Fear o' God were in him like a great light, it was. Mr Corde's a very lucky man to be allowed to step in for him over Christmas.' She nodded several times. 'Walk a few miles in the Reverend's footsteps an' he'll be the better man for it, mark my words.' She wiped half the table dry savagely, lifted the bucket on to the floor, and wiped the other half, wringing the cloth out several times.

Clarice felt defensive of Dominic, but bit her tongue rather than say anything. She took a deep breath. She needed Mrs Wellbeloved on their side. 'He seems to be a very remarkable man, even for a vicar,' she said with as much humility as she could manage.

Mrs Wellbeloved's blunt face softened. 'That he is,' she agreed more gently. 'Man of God, I say. He deserves a holiday. Go off an' do more of his paintings an' drawings, that's what he needs.' She looked Clarice up and down, and then turned away so her face was out of sight. 'Obliged you could come.' She sniffed, choking off the emotion in her voice. She picked up the bucket and threw the dirty water into the sink so hard it splashed up and a good deal of it went out again on either side, waking the cat, who shook herself angrily and curled up again.

Clarice considered whether to wipe the water up for Mrs Wellbeloved, and decided against it. Better to pretend she had not noticed. Instead she fetched Etta a dry towel for her bed and put the kettle on for another cup of tea, and then went to dust the hall – not that it needed it.

There was a sharp drop in the temperature that evening and another heavy fall of snow. Dominic banked the fires high, hoping they would stay burning most of the night, and there would at least be some warmth left in the air by morning.

Dominic looked out of his study window and saw the bleak beauty of the pale light, but he also knew it meant that no one could plough through the deep drifts to leave the village, and there would be some who would find it hard even to leave their homes to fetch food. This was where his ministry could begin. However, he had no knowledge yet at which houses he would be welcome, and he could not afford even one mistake. He was an outsider; temporarily taking the place of a man he realised was deeply loved.

So far he had only one source of information, Mrs Wellbeloved. Clarice's exact words had been, 'She has opinions about everything, which she'll share at the drop of a hat. Be busy about something else, and even if she's talking complete nonsense, for heaven's sake don't argue with her. Local knowledge is her great achievement.'

Clarice was probably right. Dominic had not had to deal with maids before, and had never considered them.

It was time he did so. He rose and went to find Clarice, who was busy in the kitchen warming two flat irons on the top of the range, ready to iron his shirts, which she had washed the day before. Cat and dog were squashed into one basket together by the stove. Dominic looked at Clarice with a deep stab of guilt. She was not beautiful in the traditional way, except for her eyes. There was far too much character in her face, too much readiness to laugh, or to lose her temper. He could not count the times she had embarrassed him. But she was also generous, and swift to forgive. She was without arrogance, and he had never known her make a promise and fail to keep it.

She could have married a man able to give her a large house and maids to look after her every need. She could have had a carriage, fashionable clothes, and invitations in society. Could she really be as happy as she seemed, face flushed, apron around her waist, testing the flat irons for temperature?

She looked up at him and smiled.

'I'm going to see Mrs Wellbeloved,' Dominic told her. 'I need her advice as to who I should call on in this weather. She'll know.'

'Excellent idea,' she approved. Then she frowned. 'Do be tactful with her, won't you She's a funny creature.'

He bit his lip to keep from laughing. 'I had noticed that, my dear.'

'Wrap up well,' she advised. 'It's bitter outside.'

'I'd noticed that too.' He kissed her quickly on the cheek, and then, before she could catch his arm, he turned and went into the hall.

He put a thick, woollen scarf around his neck, then his overcoat, gloves, and a hat. Even so he was still unprepared for the blast of cold as he opened the front door. Instead of a chill in the air as yesterday, there was a slicing wind with the cruel edge of ice on it, and the glare of light off the snow caused him to narrow his eyes. He stepped out and heard the crunch of his own footsteps. It would be very nice to change his mind and go back inside, but he could not afford to. Part of being a vicar was in not making mistakes, not listening to the tempting little voice that told you another day would do, or that there was somebody else to perform the task. He was the man people looked to here to do the work of God, and he must not fail.

He crossed the village green, seeing only a few other footprints in the thin, hard snow. The pond was partially iced over, the bench beside it deserted. The air was grey. The houses huddled down, roofs pale; thin trails of smoke smeared up against the sky. Only the blacksmith's forge glowing red looked inviting. Beyond the village, the woods were tangled branches of black, here and there denser where the evergreens clustered, pale-patched where the snow clung.

He passed an old woman with a bundle of sticks and called 'good morning' to her, but her reply was mumbled and he could not make out her words. He increased his pace and finally felt the warmth return to his body, even though his feet were numb, and he could not feel anything in his fingers but the ache of the cold.

Ten minutes later he was knocking on Mrs Wellbeloved's door, and was relieved when she opened it and invited him in. He stepped over the threshold into a dark, warm hallway smelling of floor polish and smoke.

'Well now, Mr Corde,' she said briskly. She refused to call him 'vicar'. 'What can I do for you? 'Fraid you'll have to manage the housework yourselves today. Got company coming, like I said.'

'I need your advice, Mrs Wellbeloved,' he replied, watching her expression change immediately and guarding himself from smiling.

'Ah, well that I can do, Mr Corde.' She smoothed her apron over her hips. 'What is it you need to know? Come in an' sit a moment; it's my duty to spare you that long.' She led the way into a neat front parlour where a fire was just beginning to burn up, and Mr Wellbeloved, a sturdy man with a weathered face and a shock of grey hair, was sitting whittling a piece of wood into a whistle. There was a pile of shavings on a piece of brown paper on the floor in front of him. Painted blocks were neatly stacked beside him.

When introductions were made, and he had explained that

he was carving Christmas presents for the grandchildren, Dominic asked Mrs Wellbeloved for advice about whom he should visit. He wrote down her answers, with addresses, in the notebook he had brought with him.

'An' you'd best ask Mr Boscombe to add to that,' her husband put in helpfully. 'Lives at the end o' the lane as you come in from the south. A big house with three gables. He was Vicar's right hand till about six months ago. Knew everything there was, he did.'

Mrs Wellbeloved nodded her agreement. 'That he did, an' all. Good man, Mr Boscombe. He'll see you right.'

'Until about six months ago?' Dominic questioned.

Mr Wellbeloved glared at his wife, then back at Dominic, his knife stopped in mid-air. 'That's right.'

'What happened then?'

Again they looked at each other.

'Don't know,' Mrs Wellbeloved answered. 'That'd be between Mr Boscombe and the vicar. Give up all his church duties, he did. But still a good man, an' very friendly. Nothing whatever you could take against. You go ask him. He'll tell you all as I can't.'

And Dominic had to be content with that. He thanked them and made his way reluctantly out into the bitter air again. With the directions they had given him he walked briskly the half-mile against the wind to the large, thatched house where John and Genevieve Boscombe lived with their four children.

He was welcomed in shyly, but with a gentle warmth that made him immediately comfortable. John Boscombe was a lean, quietly spoken man, with fair hair. Which was thinning a little. His wife was unusually pretty. Her skin was without blemish, her smile quick, and the fact that she was a little plump and her hair was definitely untidy seemed only to add to a sense of warmth.

Dominic heard happy laughter from upstairs, and at least three sets of feet running around. A large dog of indeterminate breed was lying on the floor in the kitchen in front of the range, and the whole room smelled of baking bread and clean linen. There was a pile of sewing in a basket, the bodice of which was obviously a doll's dress.

'What can we do for you, Vicar?' Boscombe asked. 'A cup of tea for a start? It's turned cold enough to freeze then—' he stopped, colouring faintly at a sharp look from his wife. 'Tea?' he repeated, his blue eyes wide.

'Thank you very much,' Dominic accepted.

Genevieve hastily moved a pile of folded laundry from one of the chairs and invited him to sit down at the kitchen table. He did not need the explanation that this was the only warm room in the house. People careful with money did not burn more fires than they had to. He knew that with sharp familiarity.

There was the sound of a shriek and then giggles from upstairs.

'I need your advice,' he said frankly. 'Mrs Wellbeloved

154

tells me you were very close to the vicar and could advise me as to all the people I should keep a special care for: those alone, unwell, in hard or unhappy circumstances of any kind. I'm not asking for any confidences,' he added quickly, seeing the look of anxiety in Boscombe's face. 'Only where I should begin, and whom I must not overlook.'

Boscombe frowned. 'Did the vicar not tell you those things?'

At the range, Genevieve turned to look at him, the kettle still in her hand.

'No,' Dominic said regretfully. 'I never actually met him. I was directed here by the bishop. I assume Mr Wynter advised him rather late. Perhaps his need to take a holiday arose very suddenly – a relative ill or in need? I was given no details. I was happy to come.'

'Oh!' Boscombe looked surprised, and oddly relieved. 'That was very good of you,' he added hastily. 'Yes, of course we'll both do anything we can to help.'

'Thank you. I'd like to talk to you a little about the vicar's sermons, particularly past Christmases. I don't want to repeat his words, or his exact message, but I'd like to be . . .' Suddenly he was uncertain exactly what he meant. Familiar, but original? Encouraging and new, but not disturbing? That was nonsense. He needed to make up his mind, decide between the safe and the daring. Was Christmas supposed to be safe, comfortable? Nothing more than the restating of old beliefs?

'Yes?' Boscombe prompted.

Dominic smiled self-consciously. 'Appropriate.' This short time in Cottisham mattered so much, and he was making a mess of it, being trite.

Boscombe seemed to relax. 'Of course. Anything I can tell you. But I haven't been I . . . in the vicar's confidence for the last few months. At least, not as closely as I used to be. But I'm sure I can help. What advice did Mrs Wellbeloved give you? I'll see what I can add. I've been here a while, and Genevieve was born here.'

And indeed he did, giving Dominic the colour and flavour of the village life, and in particular those who might have a need – or the reverse; be willing and able to help. He spoke of them all with kindness, but a clear-eyed view of their vulnerabilities. He also summarised several of the vicar's more notable sermons, so Dominic could be aware of their nature.

But when Dominic sat beside his own fire with Clarice that evening, hearing the wind moan in the eaves, rising shrill and more insistent, and Harry snoring gently next to the hearth, it was Boscombe's anxiety that came to his mind. He tried to explain it to her, but put into words it sounded so insubstantial – a matter of hesitations that could as easily have been shyness, or even a matter of discretion – that he felt foolish to have remembered it at all.

He asked after her day: how she was finding the house, and if the work were onerous. He knew she would say it was

156

not, whatever the truth of it. He admired her for that, and was grateful, but it only increased his sense of guilt that he could not give her the standard of comfort she had been used to before they were married.

'Oh, very good,' she said wearily. 'It's a lovely house.' She drew in her breath to add something, then changed her mind. He knew what she had been going to say – that she wished they could stay there. It was far nicer than the grim accommodation they had in London. Of course, Spindlewood and his wife had the vicarage. In the back of Dominic's mind he was always aware of how callous he had been to his first wife in the long past. He had not thought of it as a betrayal at the time, but it had been, deeply and bitterly so. Perhaps if he had been loyal to her, with or without love, she would not have been murdered.

He did not deserve such a second chance. Looking at Clarice sitting in the chair opposite him, the cat in her lap, her face grave, he was overwhelmed with gratitude.

'Except for Harry,' she said, still answering his question. 'He's fine now, but he's been sulking on the back doorstep half the day.'

'Perhaps he wanted to go out.' He started to rise to his feet.

'No, he didn't! I know enough to let a dog out now and then,' she protested. 'He'd only just come in. He sat there most of the time, or wandered around the kitchen pawing at the doors, all of them, even cupboards.'

'Could he have been hungry?' he suggested.

'Dominic! I fed him. He tries the hall cupboard and the cellar, not just the cupboards with food in. I think he really misses the vicar.'

He sat back in his chair again. 'I suppose so. I expect he'll settle. The cat's certainly happy.'

She gave him a quick smile, stroking Etta, who needled her lap happily with her claws, then went back to sleep.

Dominic leaned forward and poked the fire, sending sparks up the chimney. Clarice was right – it was a lovely house. There was almost a familiarity about it, as if at some far distant time he had lived here before and he would know instinctively where everything was. It was like coming home to some origin so far back you had forgotten you belonged here.

The third morning it was even colder. Clarice could see the village pond from the front door when Dominic went out to begin his visiting. The surface was icing over and a dusting of white snow made most of it indistinguishable from the banks. Harry went charging out into it, and had to be brought back, his chest and tummy caked with snow, and then dried off in front of the kitchen stove, loving the attention.

Clarice did not expect Mrs Wellbeloved today, and after feeding Harry and Etta, she set about the sweeping and dusting straight away, as much to keep warm and busy as for any need for it to be done. The sitting-room fire would have to be cleaned out and relit, of course, but since the ashes were still warm, it would be foolish to remove them before time. It was a waste of coal to light it simply for herself, when she could perfectly easily sit in the kitchen.

One day soon she would have to clean out the kitchen stove completely, polish the steels with emery paper, Bath brick and paraffin, black lead the iron parts and then polish them, then wash and whiten the hearthstone. But it did not have to be today. Such a job should really be begun at six in the morning, so she could get the stove set and relit in time for breakfast.

She was still thinking about it with dislike when the doorbell jangled and she went out into the hall to answer it.

A woman was standing on the step. She was muffled in a heavy cloak and had a shawl over her head, but from what Clarice could see of her, she had a handsome face and wide brown eyes, a short upper lip and round chin with extraordinary strength.

'Mrs Corde?' she enquired. She had a pleasant voice, but not the local accent.

'Yes. May I help you?'

'I rather thought I might help you,' the woman replied. 'My name is Mrs Paget. I know Mr Wynter, and I know the village quite well. I imagine many people are willing to do all they can, especially at Christmas, but you might not know who is good at which things: flowers, baking and so on.'

'Oh, thank you,' Clarice said gratefully. 'Please come in.

I would be most obliged for any advice at all.' She held the door open wide.

Mrs Paget stepped in as if it were all very familiar, and Clarice had the sudden feeling that perhaps she had been here many times. Possibly since John Boscombe had withdrawn from his church duties she had, in some practical ways, taken over.

Clarice led the way to the kitchen, explaining that she had not lit the sitting-room fire yet, and offered a cup of tea. Etta bristled at the intrusion and shot past Clarice and up the stairs. Mrs Paget gave a little cry of surprise.

'I'm sorry,' Clarice apologised. 'She's a very odd cat. I think both animals miss Mr Wynter. The dog is in and out like a fiddler's elbow, and nothing seems to satisfy the cat. I've fed her, given her milk, a warm place to lie, but she just sits there like an owl.'

'I'm afraid I don't know animals very well.' Mrs Paget arranged herself on one of the hard-backed chairs by the table, adjusting her skirts. 'I can't offer any advice. I expect you are correct and they are missing Mr Wynter. He is a wonderful man, very charming and utterly trustworthy. He knows everybody's secrets, all their private doubts and griefs, and never whispers a word to anyone. I am happy to help him in any way I can, but even to me he never gives so much as a hint of what needed to be private.'

'Admirable,' Clarice agreed, filling the kettle and setting it on the hob. 'And absolutely necessary. All I really would like to know is who is gifted at what practical skill – and of course who is not!' She gave Mrs Paget a quick smile.

'Oh, quite!' Mrs Paget eased quickly, sinking back with a flash of understanding. 'That can be every bit as much a disaster. At all costs avoid Mrs Lampeter's baking, and Mrs Porter's soup! Never give Mrs Unsworth the flowers. She only has to touch lilies and they go brown.'

They both laughed, and settled to discuss matters of skill, tact, need and general usefulness. Harry remained sulking in the corner, and Etta never reappeared.

Dominic returned for luncheon, and went out again. Clarice spent the afternoon going through various cupboards, seeing what polishes, brushes and so on she could find, and if she could repack them a little more tidily so as to make more room. It was annoying to open a cupboard door and have the contents slide out around your feet, or worse, fall on top of you from the shelf above.

In the middle of the afternoon she cleaned out and lit the fire in the sitting room to be warm when Dominic came home. He was bound to be frozen. Earlier she had made hot soup – better, she hoped, that Mrs Porter's!

She was tidying the bookshelves behind the sofa in the sitting room when she came across a leather-bound Bible. Its pages were gold-edged, but very well used, as if it were someone's personal possession, rather than one for general reference. She opened it and saw the vicar's name in it on the front page, and dated some fifty years ago. She ruffled the pages, and saw tiny handwritten notes in the margins, particularly in the Book of Isaiah, and in the four Gospels of the New Testament. She had to carry them to the window for enough light to read them. They were very personal. There was a passion and an honesty in them that made her stop reading. They were too intimate; a man's reminder to himself, not to others.

She stood in the fading winter sun, the light greying outside, the fire burning up behind her. Why had he not taken this with him? An accidental omission, surely? It did not belong in this room: in his bedroom, if not with him. He must have left it out to pack, and somehow overlooked it.

She should find his address and send it on to him. The postal service was good; it would get to him in a day or two at the outside. Her mind made up, she went into the study, and looked for the address of Mr Wynter's holiday dwelling. It took her only ten minutes. She was surprised: it was an area of Norfolk she knew quite well, with beautiful wide skies and open beaches facing the North Sea. It would be a wonderful place for him to create more of his pictures. It was famous for its artists. She smiled, imagining him drinking in its splendour, and then striving to capture it on paper.

Then she read the address again. It was a small hotel in one of the seaside villages. But she had been there herself two years ago – and the hotel was closed, turned into a private house. He could not be there. It must be a mistake, an address from a previous holiday – although she had seen no pictures in the house that could be from that region. She would have to put on her coat and boots and go and ask Mrs Wellbeloved. No doubt she would have the correct address. She must send him his scriptures.

But Mrs Wellbeloved had no idea where the vicar was, if he were not at that hotel. She was very sorry, and not a little annoyed also to have been misled. Clarice should try Sir Peter, who might know on account of church business. She could think of no one else.

Long Spoon Lane

Anne Perry

Early one morning, two bombs explode in an East London street. Thomas Pitt of the Special Branch arrives in time to chase the bombers to a run-down tenement in Long Spoon Lane. There, two men are arrested and one shot dead – but who and where is the killer?

Starting to investigate, Pitt uncovers a web of corruption within the police force, and all the clues point to Superintendent Wetron of Bow Street as its mastermind. But Wetron has allies in ever sphere, making it almost impossible to pin guilt to him.

Anxieties roused by the bombings are being fanned by the press, and a bill to arm the London police is about to be rushed through Parliament. Then Pitt's most deadly enemy, Sir Charles Voisey, approaches him proposing they join forces to prevent Wetron becoming the most powerful man in England. And in spite of the danger this involves, Pitt has to agree.

Anne Perry has pulled out all the stops for this breathtaking tale of passion, principle and skulduggery, written with her unrivalled skill at evoking the world of Victorian England.

Acclaim for Anne Perry's writing:

'Brilliantly presented, ingeniously developed and packed with political implications that reverberate on every level of British society' *New York Times Book Review*

'A complex plot supported by superb storytelling' *Scotland on Sunday*

'A beautifully written work of psychological depth and poetic resonance . . . it is compelling from start to finish' *Lady*

0 7553 2057 3

headline

ANNE PERRY

Shoulder the Sky

In April 1915 Joseph Reavley is serving as chaplain on the Front Line at Ypres. The War that should have been 'over by Christmas' has already decimated the British Expeditionary Force. To Joseph's sector comes an ambitious young war correspondent determined to expose the horrors of trench life. But before he can dispatch his piece, he is found dead in no-man's-land. Still seeking the man behind his parents' murder, and to protect his sister Judith from the pain of an impossible romance, Joseph must find the truth. His search takes him to London and the beaches of Gallipoli, and at last to face a desperate moral judgement which challenges every belief he holds.

SHOULDER THE SKY is the second novel in Anne Perry's insightful and hard-hitting quintet charting the English experience of the First World War.

'The elegance of the prose and depth of characterisation combine to create a powerful and poignant journey into the past' *The Lady*

Praise for Anne Perry's other historical fiction:

'A complex plot supported by superb storytelling' *Scotland on Sunday*

'Brilliantly presented, ingeniously developed and packed with political implications that reverberate on every level of British society' *New York Times*

'Perry's characters are richly drawn and the plot [is] satisfyingly serpentine' *Booklist*

0 7553 0287 7

R

headline
review

A Christmas Journey

Anne Perry

A tranquil weekend party at a magnificent country house in early December is shattered by a suspicious death.

Isobel Alvie makes a cruel remark about Gwendolen Kilmuir on the night Gwendolen is expected to become engaged to the eligible Bertie Rosythe. The next morning Gwendolen's body is found in the ornamental lake on the estate. It appears she has thrown herself from the bridge.

The other guests hold Isobel morally guilty of causing Gwendolen's death and threaten to exclude her from society in future, which would mean ruin for her. The host, Omegus Jones, suggests that in total expiation of her sin, Isobel should carry Gwendolen's final letter to her mother in the far north of Scotland.

Realising that the journey will be both physically and emotionally arduous for Isobel, Lady Vespasia Cumming-Gould resolves to accompany her. The two women find their Christmas pilgrimage brings answers to some unexpected and profound questions.

A CHRISTMAS JOURNEY is a delightful Christmas novella from the internationally bestselling author Anne Perry.

'This brief work has an almost Jamesian subtlety, and with its powerful message of responsibility and redemption . . . it conveys a moral force in keeping with the season' *Wall Street Journal*

Acclaim for Anne Perry's novels:

'The novel has a totally contemporary feel and is admirably well-written' *Guardian*

0 7553 2115 4

headline

Now you can buy any of these other bestselling books by **Anne Perry** from your bookshop or *direct from her publisher*.

FREE P&P AND UK DELIVERY
(Overseas and Ireland £3.50 per book)

Thomas Pitt series

Long Spoon Lane	£6.99
Seven Dials	£6.99
Southampton Row	£6.99
The Whitechapel Conspiracy	£6.99
Half Moon Street	£6.99

William Monk series

The Shifting Tide	£6.99
Death of a Stranger	£6.99
A Funeral in Blue	£6.99
Slaves and Obsession	£6.99
The Twisted Root	£6.99

World War I series

Angels in the Gloom	£6.99
Shoulder the Sky	£6.99
No Graves as Yet	£6.99

Other novels

A Christmas Visitor	£6.99
A Christmas Journey	£6.99
Come Armageddon	£6.99
Tathea	£6.99

TO ORDER SIMPLY CALL THIS NUMBER

01235 400 414

or visit our website: www.madaboutbooks.com

Prices and availability subject to change without notice.